"It was what was called a chacmool..."

EMPIRE OF THE SKULL

I of

D0712050

6/8/2009

Philip Caveney

Also by Philip Caveney:

Alec Devlin: The Eye of the Serpent

Sebastian Darke: Prince of Fools
Sebastian Darke: Prince of Pirates
Sebastian Darke: Prince of Explorers

EMPIRE OF THE SKULL

ALEC DEVLIN

PHILIP CAVENEY

RED FOX
In association with The Bodley Head

THE EMPIRE OF THE SKULL
A RED FOX BOOK 978 1 862 30637 0

First published in Great Britain by Red Fox,
an imprint of Random House Children's Books
A Random House Group Company

This edition published 2009

1 3 5 7 9 10 8 6 4 2

The Random House Group Limited supports the Forest Stewardship Council
(FSC), the leading international forest certification organization.
All our titles that are printed on Greenpeace-approved FSC-certified
paper carry the FSC logo. Our paper procurement policy
can be found at www.rbooks.co.uk/environment.

Set in Bembo 14/17pt
by Falcon Oast Graphic Art Ltd.

Red Fox Books are published by Random House Children's Books,
61–63 Uxbridge Road, London W5 5SA

www.kidsatrandomhouse.co.uk
www.rbooks.co.uk

Addresses for companies within The Random House Group Limited can be found at:
www.randomhouse.co.uk/offices.htm

THE RANDOM HOUSE GROUP Limited Reg. No. 954009

A CIP catalogue record for this book is available from the British Library.

Printed and bound in Great Britain by
CPI Bookmarque, Croydon, CR0 4TD

*For Ray Bradbury, the man who made me
want to be a writer . . . and for Tony,
who has worked so hard to spread
the word.*

Mexico 1924
Itztli came forward onto the platform at the top of the gigantic step pyramid and held up the obsidian dagger. A cry of exaltation went up from the people in the plaza below and he gazed down upon them, his features set in a benevolent smile. As always at such times, he was shocked to see how few of them were left. Over the past few years, many had succumbed to sickness, and it seemed to him that fewer children were being born than at any time in the city's history. But Mictlantecuhtli had spoken to him in a dream a few nights earlier. The god had told him that

more sacrifices were needed if the city of Colotlán were to return to its former glory. Today, the lord of Mictlan's demands would be met in full. The black dagger would do its work and fresh blood would spill down the steps of the great pyramid.

His name meant 'obsidian', the hard volcanic stone from which the Aztecs fashioned their knives. He was a high priest of the city, the most powerful of them all. He had risen to his position by displaying total commitment to the god to which this sacred building and the city itself were dedicated – Mictlantecuhtli, the god of the dead, the all-powerful lord of Mictlan, the lowest section of the underworld. Behind Itztli towered a huge statue of the god, depicted as a skeleton, the skull impossibly large on the body, its teeth set in a mirthless grin. The skeleton's arms were extended as though to welcome the souls of the slain into his protection; and from the open maw of the great flue beyond the statue, heat rose steadily into the sky.

Lately, the lord of Mictlan had been expressing his displeasure by spewing smoke and ash from his underworld domain; occasionally great roars had shaken the very ground upon which his city stood. Itztli knew that the god was demanding yet more sacrifices. Beneath the statue's feet stood the blood-stained altar where these sacrifices, both animal and human, were regularly made.

But first the crowd needed to be prepared. The high priest strode backwards and forwards on the platform, his arms raised, his expression jubilant. He smiled down at his people and let his voice ring out loud and clear.

'Let the ceremony begin!'

Below him, they cheered him on, eager for the blood-letting to start. This was a joyous occasion and they shouted their encouragement. Vendors moved through the crowd selling *pulque*, the powerful beer made from fermented cactus juice, along with peanuts, sweet potatoes and corn pancakes. Crowds of children ran around, shouting and playing their pretend battles.

Itztli glanced across at the emperor, who sat on a gilded throne. Chicahua. The name meant 'strong', but for all the fine ornamentation he wore – the quetzal-feather headdress, the golden earrings, the fine cloak, nothing could hide the truth. He was a rather podgy twelve-year-old boy, so short that with his fat bottom on the throne, his sandaled feet didn't even touch the flagstones. He was being fed cocoa beans by his servant, Patli, and he looked bored, as though he would rather be anywhere else. On the other side of the throne stood his elder sister, Tepin, who accompanied her little brother everywhere and had more influence over him than the high priest would have liked.

Itztli worked hard to hide his resentment. The boy had come to power only because earlier that year, his father, Ahcautli, had contracted a fever and died. Chicahua was not the first child emperor among the Aztec people, nor would he be the last. But what a tragedy it was that he should have turned out to be such a weakling, a boy who thought of sweets and toys and not much else, a boy who always looked to his sister for guidance. Itztli feared for the city if such a boy were left in control; deep in his heart he knew that he could not allow such a situation to continue for long. Little wonder that the lord of Mictlan was so angry. Many of Itztli's fellow priests had whispered to him that he was the true power in the city; that he was the one who should be giving the orders. But he knew that he must bide his time and wait for the right moment.

For now, there were the demands of his god to be satisfied. The high priest looked at the waiting captives, naked save for loincloths. They were bound together with ropes; trembling and weeping as the moment of their deliverance approached. These were ignorant natives from some far-flung jungle village, taken prisoner by Colotlán's jaguar warriors. With each passing year they were obliged to wander further and further through the rainforests in search of suitable victims.

Itztli lifted a hand and gestured to two priests waiting a short distance away. They wore masks, one of Mictlantecuhtli himself, the other of Quetzalcoatl, the feathered serpent, the god of civilization. Itztli preferred not to wear a mask. He liked his victims to look upon his real face as he dispatched them; to see the cold venom in his eyes. At his command, the other priests gestured to the guards to release one of the captives. The rope was cut and a man, a thin, dark-skinned fellow with a bone nose-plug and shell ornaments in his earlobes, was pushed forward. The priests each took one of his arms and led him towards the altar.

He was so terrified he could hardly stay upright. His eyes were wide and staring and his mouth hung open as though his jaw had lost all its strength. He was mumbling something over and over – no doubt praying to some obscure jungle god. He knew his time was at hand and was asking that his journey to the underworld be an easy one.

Itztli stepped back and the two priests brought the man over to the low stone altar and laid him on his back. They held his arms out to each side, so he could not struggle. He was gasping for breath, but he continued to pray as Itztli moved back to stand over him. The high priest looked upwards and raised the obsidian dagger, the jagged black blade glinting in the sunlight.

'Great Quetzalcoatl, Lord of the Sky!' he cried. 'Guide my hand. May this first sacrifice find favour with Mictlantecuhtli.'

He looked down at the prisoner's chest, selecting just the right spot, then lifted the dagger and brought it down hard. He gave a quick horizontal thrust, opening up the chest, and plunged his free hand inside to grasp the still beating heart. A second knife thrust released the heart from its fleshy home and he lifted it in his bloody hand so that the crowd could see it. A great roar of approval rose up, drowning out the terrified gasps of his victim, who was staring up at his own heart in mute terror, his whole body shaking with the shock.

But then the finisher stepped forward, his machete raised, and one swift stroke took the victim's head from his body. The finisher lifted it by the hair for everyone to see, displaying it to every section of the crowd. Then he flung it down the steps of the pyramid. Eager helpers ran forward to catch it and place it on the skull rack. A few moments later, the headless body was thrown down another flight of steps like discarded rubbish, of no worth now that the all-powerful heart had been removed.

Now, from the other captives, came wails of despair, for there was no doubting the fate that lay in store for them.

Itztli threw the heart onto a brazier of hot coals and breathed in the smell of burning flesh. Then he strode forward again, his bloody hands raised in front of the crowd. He knew that they both loved and feared him. Loved him because they knew that he was their guide to the ways of the gods. Feared him because they realized how easily they might find themselves on the sharp end of that deadly obsidian blade.

The high priest gestured to the guards and a second captive was released, this time an older man, powerfully muscled and carrying the tribal scars that spoke of his position within his tribe. Unlike the first man he seemed unafraid; he came forward without hesitation and looked Itztli in the eye, as though challenging him to do his worst. The high priest favoured the man with a mirthless smile, telling himself that such bravery would quickly evaporate when the man found himself looking at his own beating heart. Then he moved back and allowed the two priests to stretch the warrior across the sacrificial stone.

He stepped forward and raised the knife. He looked to the heavens again. 'Great Quetzalcoatl!' he roared. 'Show us that you approve of our sacrifice. Give us a sign so that we might understand.'

And then there was a noise in the sky – a strange rumbling that turned into a continuous roar that seemed to fill the heavens with its power. This was surely not the thunder of Mictlan. Far below Itztli, the cheers of the crowd changed to gasps of astonishment. He saw that people were tilting back their heads to gaze upwards; some of them were pointing at the clouds.

Itztli lowered his dagger and looked up, and a gasp spilled unbidden from his lips. Something was crossing the sky just above his head, something he at first took to be a huge bird. But he soon saw that this was not a thing of bone and flesh and feathers but something that men had made. Its wings were static, outstretched, not moving up and down as bird's would; its hard body glittered in the sunlight as though made of metal. It was knifing downwards at a steep angle, and as Itztli watched, the noise faltered, making a series of spluttering coughs.

Down in the crowd, the sounds of amazement quickly became shouts of fear: this was something that none of them could understand. People began to run in all directions, their blood-lust forgotten.

The dagger dropped from Itztli's hand as he lost himself in the wonder of the moment; and even the intended victim was sitting up, staring at the mystifying thing as it passed overhead. The high priest was not afraid. He realized that this was not the sign he had asked for, and there was no use pretending that it was a good omen. The arrival of this man-made thing was an insult, timed to interrupt a most solemn occasion. The lord of Mictlan would be angry and prompt action needed to be taken. Itztli could see that whatever this strange apparition was, it could not stay airborne for much longer. As it flew over the city, it was dropping lower and lower in the sky. From where he stood at the top of the pyramid, he could see it long after it must have passed out of the sight of the people below. It was moving on across the rainforest; at any moment it would disappear into the green depths that lay all around. He waited, and for a few moments there was a deep silence.

Then he heard it. The distant crashing of vegetation as the huge sky chariot ploughed into the forest. It sounded like the end of the world. On the horizon he saw great clouds of birds whirling up from the trees and the noise seemed to go on for a very long time; finally it stopped and everything was silent again.

Itztli looked down at what was left of the crowd below. Those who had not fled were looking hopefully up at him, expecting him to take control. He glanced at Chicahua. The boy was sitting on his oversized throne, his mouth open, revealing several partially chewed cocoa beans sitting on his tongue. He looked rigid with terror; beside him, Patli wasn't much better, his wizened features showing an expression of dismay. The boy's sister was merely staring at the place where the sky chariot had vanished, as though mesmerized. No point in expecting any help from that direction.

Itztli turned and beckoned to Tlaloc, the leader of the jaguar warriors who policed the city. The tall, muscular figure hurried forward.

'My lord?' he enquired.

'Take your best men and find the place where the great bird came down,' the high priest ordered. 'Bring back anything of interest you find there.'

'Yes, my lord.' Tlaloc bowed his head respectfully and Itztli could tell that he was frightened.

'Do not be afraid,' he said. 'It is men who have dared to do this thing.'

'But that sky machine, my lord — surely that must be the work of wizards?'

Itztli shook his head. 'It is but a thing that men have made — and all men must yield to my knife and the word of our god. Now, go, find whoever has done this and bring them to me.'

Tlaloc nodded and then gestured to the prisoner, who was still sitting on the altar, looking dazed. 'What of this man, my lord?' he asked.

Itztli glanced at him. In all the excitement, he had quite forgotten about his intended victim. 'Put him back with the others and lock them away,' he said. 'Our ceremony has been defiled. We'll postpone it until we have found the ones responsible for such an outrage.'

'Very good, my lord.'

A guard took the prisoner by the arm and dragged him back to his companions. They were led down the steps, still roped together, their expressions stunned, no doubt amazed to find that, against all the odds, they were still alive.

'Itztli!' The high priest turned to find Chicahua gazing fearfully up at him. 'What does it mean?' he gasped. 'Is it the end of the world?'

Itztli smiled and tried not to picture himself putting his hands around the boy's throat and choking the life out of him. 'Your highness, it's nothing to be concerned about,' he purred. He gestured at the huge stone skull that towered above them, its sightless eyes staring out across the plaza. 'The lord of Mictlan saw that thing in his heavens and sent Quetzalcoatl, the feathered serpent, to tear it from the sky. Men must have been behind that abomination; if they survived, we will find them and give them as gifts to the lord of Mictlan. There is nothing to fear. Nothing at all.'

He bent down and picked up his dagger from the pool of blood in which it lay. He bowed respectfully to the emperor; then descended the steps of the pyramid.

CHAPTER ONE

The Olmec Head

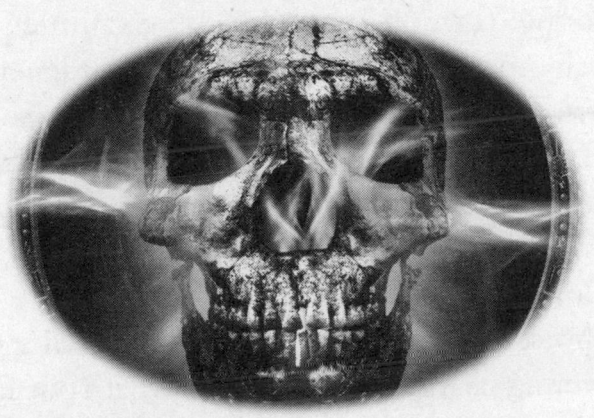

Alec Devlin squeezed his horse's flanks gently with his legs and urged it over the crest of the ridge and into the thickly wooded valley below. He had been a confident rider from an early age and rarely had a problem getting a mount to obey him. Coates, his valet, on the other hand, had never been comfortable on horseback and was having a job controlling his big chestnut mare. He sat awkwardly in his saddle, looking faintly ridiculous in khaki shirt and trousers, with a straw sombrero shading his ruddy features.

'How much further, Master Alec?' he shouted.

'When you announced this little trip, you gave no indication that we were going to ride this far.'

'It's only a little way further,' Alec assured him, without turning round. He examined the sketchy map that Pablo, his father's gardener, had drawn for him, and had to admit that it gave no real indication of distance. But they had been riding for hours and he was fairly sure it couldn't be much further.

Coates dug his heels in and managed to urge his horse forward until he was riding alongside his young charge. 'I don't know what your father would say if he knew we'd come all the way out here,' he complained in his strong Yorkshire accent. 'You made it sound as though it was just down the road, but we've been riding for hours.'

Alec sighed. He was well aware that he had tricked Coates into making this trip, but the truth was he had been bored out of his mind sitting around his father's hacienda in Veracruz, and when Pablo had mentioned that an amazing antiquity was to be seen just a few hours to the south, he was determined to see it.

Alec's father had been transferred from the Egyptian embassy in Cairo the previous autumn, and he, Alec and Coates had spent several months in the hustle and bustle of Mexico City. But then, in the New Year, his father had been sent to Veracruz, away to the south, and the three of them had found themselves in a completely different environment. Here the wide dusty plains gave way to lush equatorial rainforest. In the absence of a suitable school, a home tutor was found for Alec — Señor Vargas, who spoke excellent English but managed to make every subject seem as dull as ditchwater.

At first Alec had pined for his beloved Egypt; but he had quickly realized that Mexico had its own incredible history, complete with priceless relics, pyramids and ancient sites. And so it was that he began to immerse himself in books about the Aztec, Mayan and Olmec civilizations. And when, a few days earlier, his father had been temporarily recalled to Mexico City, Alec had spotted an opportunity to do more than read about it in textbooks.

Now here he was, riding through dense woodland, close to his objective, and feeling the old excitement flooding back.

Coates, meanwhile, was far from happy. 'If you'd only been content to wait a few more days,

Master Alec, perhaps Mr Wade would have been here,' he said.

Alec raised his eyebrows. 'I'm amazed to hear you say that,' he replied. 'I understood that you didn't *like* Ethan Wade.'

'I'd be the first to admit that he's not my favourite person. But at the same time, he's a useful man to have around in a sticky situation.'

They rode on in silence for a while. Alec had first met the tall American at his Uncle Will's archaeological dig in the Valley of the Kings near Luxor. After Uncle Will's sudden illness and the mysterious disappearance of his young assistant, Ethan had been obliged to oversee the dig, even though he would have been the first to admit that he was not really qualified for the job. He and Alec had immediately struck up a close friendship, but Coates had made no secret of the fact that he found Ethan reckless and over-bearing, an impression that was not diminished by the terrifying adventure that had followed.

So he hadn't been pleased when, a few weeks back, Alec's father had announced that he had decided to engage Ethan's services as a family bodyguard. Mexico was still a lawless place, he had pointed out, and Ethan's experiences as a hired gun in Montana would prove useful. Alec had been delighted at this news, and when a telegram had alerted them to his imminent arrival, he had been over the moon. But a week had passed and still there was no sign of him. Alec had been simply too impatient to wait any longer.

'I think we should head back,' said Coates anxiously. 'I really do.'

Alec kept his horse moving briskly through the trees. 'I don't know what you're so worried about,' he said. 'The revolution's officially over. President Obregón is in control now.'

'Hmm. I wonder if anybody has bothered to tell the Mexican people that?' muttered Coates grimly. 'You know what it can be like in these parts. Bandits round every corner. Obregón only came to power by overthrowing the last president and he still has plenty of enemies. Why do you suppose your father decided to engage the services of Mr Wade in the first place?'

It was a good question and one for which Alec had no ready answer. His horse emerged from the cover of the trees onto a stretch of hilly grassland. He reined in and stared at what was waiting for them up ahead. Coates, head down as he struggled with the reins, continued to complain.

'And has it occurred to you, Master Alec, that Pablo is not the most reliable of people? I mean, for goodness' sake, he's only a humble gardener. I've no idea why you would choose to put your faith in— Oh.'

Coates reined his horse in too and they sat looking at what lay ahead of them on the grass. It was a huge grey stone head, some eight or nine feet high, depicting a man wearing a close-fitting helmet. He had distinctive features – a wide splayed nose and thick, shapely lips. His earlobes were pierced, as though awaiting the delivery of some giant stone earrings. There was nothing below the chin – no indication of neck or shoulders. The head sat on the grass as though it had dropped from heaven.

'Good Lord,' said Coates quietly. 'When you said we were going to look for a head, I had no idea you meant . . . It's *huge!*'

Alec nodded. He clicked his tongue and urged his horse forward. Coates followed. It wasn't until they drew closer that they could appreciate the sheer size of the thing. Alec dismounted, hitched the horse's reins to a stunted tree and went forward to touch the sculpture. Even standing on tiptoe he could reach no higher than the warrior's forehead. He turned and smiled at Coates. 'Now tell me you think Pablo's map is inaccurate,' he said.

'All right, point taken. Nobody likes hearing "I told you so."'

Alec grinned. He went back to his horse, and reaching into a saddlebag, took out a folding seat, his sketchbook and some pencils. He walked around the head for a while, choosing the best angle, then sat down and with swift, deft movements began to sketch out the shape of it.

Coates dismounted clumsily, tethered his mare and began to remove items from his own saddlebags. He unfolded a plaid blanket, which he laid out on the grass, then unhooked a wicker picnic hamper from the back of his saddle. He set this carefully on the blanket and began to unpack the contents.

Alec glanced up from his work and gave a snort of disbelief. 'A picnic?' he asked incredulously.

'Of course, Master Alec. Just because we're out in the wilds, it doesn't mean we have to go hungry.' Coates paused for a moment and studied the stone head. 'So that would be . . . Aztec?' he enquired.

'Olmec,' Alec corrected him. 'Much older. The Aztec empire flourished around twelve to thirteen hundred AD . . . only around six hundred years ago. This head dates from between twelve hundred and four hundred *BC*. The Olmecs were the first of the great Mexican civilizations. The truth is, we don't really know very much about them.'

Coates smiled and went back to arranging the picnic things. 'I must say, Master Alec, coming out with you is a regular education. You've obviously been doing your homework.'

Alec shrugged. He was sketching in the eyes and nose now, trying to capture the essence of those distinctive carved features. 'Well, since we can't be in Egypt, I decided to investigate what's right on our doorstep.'

Coates frowned. 'Let's hope we don't uncover anything like the horrors we found in the Valley of the Kings,' he said. 'You know, we never really gave your father the full story of what happened out there.'

'That's probably just as well. He'd be likely to have us both committed to an institution.'

Alec thought back for a moment. It all seemed so long ago. Now he was a year older and a year closer to his goal of being a full-time archae-ologist. In the meantime, there was Señor Vargas and his interminable lessons: annoyingly, when-ever Alec asked him questions about the history of his own country, his answers were vague. It seemed ridiculous that the man had a good working knowledge of the French Revolution and the American War of Independence, but knew next to nothing about his own ancestors.

'Would you care to have a break for a mug of tea and a salmon and cucumber sandwich?' asked Coates. And then, when Alec burst out laughing, he added, 'I fail to see the humour in the situation.'

'Only you, Coates,' spluttered Alec. 'In the middle of this wilderness, with a thumping great Olmec head in front of us, only *you* would be carrying salmon and cucumber sandwiches!'

Coates frowned. 'Well, at least I was thinking ahead, Master Alec. If it had been left to you, we'd be out here without even a canteen of water. Sometimes I fear you are far too impetuous for your own good.'

Alec chuckled. 'Lucky I've got you, eh, Coates? And by the way . . .'

'Yes?'

'I know I've asked you this before, but now I've turned sixteen, do you think we could skip the "Master Alec" routine?'

Coates smiled enigmatically and held out a plate of sandwiches.

Alec sighed and laid down his sketchbook. 'I suppose I *am* a bit peckish,' he admitted. He got up and took one of the dainty sandwiches, then crammed the whole thing into his mouth.

'Chew every mouthful thirty-two times,' Coates advised him. 'I've always observed that motto and I have perfect digestion.' He poured tea from his Thermos flask into two enamel mugs and added milk from a small bottle. He passed one up to Alec, then grimaced as he sipped his own. 'Doesn't taste the same when it's not served in bone china,' he observed. 'But cups and saucers would have got broken in those saddlebags.'

'Don't worry,' Alec assured him. 'I shan't tell anyone you drank from a tin mug. Your secret is safe with me.' He turned and gazed back at the stone head. 'Imagine,' he said. 'Carving that with nothing but primitive chisels. How long must it have taken them? And of course, the other question: how did they get a piece of basalt that weighs more than twenty tons way out here?' He gestured around at the rolling hills. 'The nearest source is fifty miles away.'

'It's certainly a mystery,' admitted Coates. He looked around. 'Perhaps they could have—'

He broke off suddenly and Alec glanced at him.

'What's wrong?' he asked.

Coates was gazing back the way they had come. Two horsemen were riding slowly over the ridge towards them. They descended the hill and disappeared into the trees.

CHAPTER TWO

Trouble with a Capital T

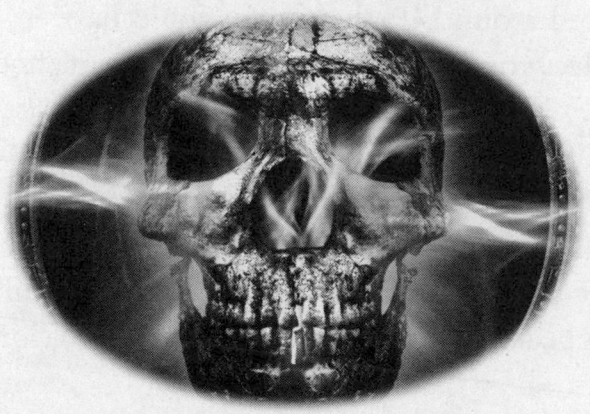

When they emerged from the wood, it became evident that the two riders were Mexicans. One man wore a sombrero, the other a serape, a colourful fringed shawl; and as they drew closer, Alec could see that they both had guns and holsters slung around their waists. The man in the sombrero carried a leather bandolier studded with bullets. They glinted in the sunlight as he approached.

'I don't like the look of these two,' murmured Coates uneasily. 'They look like trouble with a capital T.'

'You shouldn't judge a book by its cover,' said

Alec; but he had to admit that there was a certain degree of menace in the way the men rode, their shoulders hunched, their grubby faces expressionless.

They reined in their horses a short distance away and sat there, studying Alec and Coates in silence for a few moments. Then the man wearing the bandolier grinned, displaying large white teeth, his gold fillings glinting below his moustache. Alec distrusted him immediately: the grin had no warmth to it; he was just baring his teeth. The man was tall and wiry; his partner in the serape was thicker set and had dark stubble on his chin.

'*Buenos días, amigos,*' said Bandolier. 'It's a fine day but you are a long way from home, I think.'

'Not so very far,' said Coates quietly. 'Actually, we're with a much bigger party, some twenty men or so. They're following us. Should be here any moment.'

Bandolier grinned. 'Isn't that strange?' he said. 'We too are with a big crowd. They are back up the trail a little way. They send us ahead to scout out the land. Hey, you know what? Maybe our friends will run into your friends.' He turned and said something to his companion in rapid

Spanish. Serape gave a harsh laugh and a brief reply.

'He says it will be quite a party,' said Bandolier. His mocking gaze moved to examine the picnic rug and the hamper. 'Oh, but forgive me – it looks like you were having your dinner.'

'That's all right,' said Alec. He picked up a plate of sandwiches, smiling in what he hoped was a friendly manner. He knew that in such circumstance it was important not to appear afraid. 'Perhaps we could offer you a sandwich,' he said.

Bandolier looked at the plate, his eyes narrowed as though he suspected Alec were trying to poison him. Then he reached out a filthy hand and picked up one of the sandwiches between thumb and nicotine-stained forefinger. He lifted the sandwich and sniffed at it dubiously. 'What is this?' he asked.

'Salmon and cucumber,' Coates assured him. 'Made them this morning. Absolutely delicious, though I say so myself.'

Alec moved round to the other horse and held out the plate but Serape just grunted and shook his head. Bandolier took a bite of his sandwich, chewed for a moment and then spat it out.

'Gringo food,' he said. 'Tastes like dog.' He flung the remains of the sandwich aside.

'How kind of you to say,' muttered Coates. 'And such charming manners.' He glanced at Alec, his eyes warning him to step away from the men.

Alec did just that, returning to the blanket and setting the plate down. He looked across at the tethered horses, remembering that Coates carried a pistol in one of the saddlebags and wondering if he could get to it before Bandolier noticed. He took a step forward but the Mexican's voice stopped him in his tracks.

'Hey, kid, where you going?'

Alec turned back, still trying to keep the smile on his face. 'I, er . . . have something in my saddlebags I . . . wanted to give you,' he said. 'A present.' He thought for a moment, trying to imagine something the Mexican might want. 'A . . . bottle of whisky?'

Bandolier looked at him in disgust. 'You gringos,' he said. 'You think we Mexicans will roll over and beg if you offer us a drink. I am not stupid, you know.'

'I never said you were,' said Alec. He was trying to remain calm but he was horribly aware of a trickle of sweat running slowly down his spine. 'And for your information, we're not *gringos*. We are English.'

Bandolier shrugged as though this was of no concern to him. 'You are all the same to me,' he said. 'You come to this country and think you own it. I got news for you, kid, you don' own nothing. You hear me? Nothing.' Now he was studying the Olmec head as though he had only just noticed it. 'What are you doing here?' he asked. 'Don' you know this is dangerous territory to be out alone?'

'I was drawing the head,' said Alec, pointing. 'I'm interested in archaeology, you see. It's Olmec – it's thousands of years old.' He moved across and picked up his sketchbook. 'See? I'm making a drawing of it.'

'So I see,' said Bandolier, but it was evident he wasn't interested. He seemed to be deliberating.

'You . . . you speak very good English,' said Alec, trying to fight down the tight knot of fear that was coiling in his stomach. 'Where did you learn it?'

Bandolier rolled his eyes. 'I was *vaquero* for a gringo rancher for many years,' he said. 'I guess I picked it up, mostly from listening to him give orders. He liked to give the orders, you understand? Always he picked me for the worst jobs. I worked for him longer than anyone, but he didn't cut me no favours. In the end I got tired of being pushed around. Figured I'd make my own way. But before I rode out, I left him something to remember me by.' He laughed unpleasantly.

Alec wasn't sure what that something might have been but was fairly sure it wouldn't have been a nice bunch of flowers.

Bandolier looked contemptuously at the sketchbook for a moment. 'An artist, huh?' he asked at last. 'Where you from, kid?'

'Veracruz,' said Alec.

'You got people there?'

'My father. He . . . he works with the British embassy.'

Alec was aware of Coates directing a fierce glare in his direction, as though warning him not to mention his father. But it was too late now.

'Yeah?' Bandolier seemed to brighten at this news. Again he turned and said something to Serape. The second man considered for a moment and then nodded. Bandolier turned back to Alec. 'He's a big man in Veracruz, eh? I bet he's worth a lot of pesos. And I bet he's real proud of his boy. Hey, you know what I'm thinking?'

There was a silence.

'I can't imagine,' said Alec at last.

'I think maybe this man would pay much money to have his son back again in one piece.'

It was obvious where this was leading. Alec felt a growing sense of panic but stubbornly refused to let it show. 'My father is poor,' he said. 'They don't pay him very much.'

Bandolier laughed derisively. 'Yeah, sure, kid. And I'm Pancho Villa!'

'Listen,' said Coates, and Alec heard an unfamiliar note of desperation in his valet's voice. 'It's been very nice chatting with you, *señor*, but I would advise you and your friend to ride on. Master Alec's father is a close friend of President Obregón. If anything should happen to us, I wouldn't want to be in your boots.'

Bandolier turned his head to one side and spat dismissively. 'Obregón? You think I care about him? He's just another jumped-up *norteño* with big ideas. Me and my *compadres*, we don' look out for nobody but us. We see something we want, we take it. I think maybe you two ride along with us. Maybe we send a message to the boy's father in Veracruz.' He thought for a moment. 'Maybe we take a knife and cut off one of his ears, send that to him and ask him for one hundred thousand pesos.'

'Now look here—' said Coates.

'No, you look at me, Señor Englishman. You look in my eyes and know that I am not kidding around here. You are coming with us.'

'We're going nowhere,' Coates insisted. 'I'm warning you—'

'You're *warning* me?' Bandolier laughed again. 'Excuse me, but you are the one standing there with no gun. Don't you tell me what is happening. It could be I decide just to take the boy and leave you here for the buzzards to pick at. What d'you think of that, Señor Englishman?'

Coates was about to step forward but Alec's voice stilled him: 'Don't be silly, Coates. He wouldn't hesitate to shoot you.'

Coates turned and glared at Alec. 'Didn't I warn you this was a lawless country?' he said. 'Now look at the mess you've got us into. Perhaps in future you'll think before you act.'

Alec felt bad. It was true, he had risked so much coming out here, and now it had all gone disastrously wrong. 'I'm sorry, Coates,' he said. 'I really didn't think it was that dangerous. I just so wanted to see the head, I—'

'Hey!' snapped Bandolier. 'I don' got all day to sit around listening to you two!' He said something to Serape, who spurred his horse over to the other mounts and started to search through the saddlebags. In a few moments his hand emerged holding Coates's pistol.

'Oh, now ain't that funny,' said Bandolier. 'I thought you said that was a bottle of whisky.' He studied Alec intently. 'You lie to me again, kid, and I will take a stick and beat you till you scream for mercy. You got that? Now, both of you get on your horses and come along with us.'

Alec thought for a moment. 'Can I just get my sketching things?' he asked.

Bandolier looked as though he was about to explode. 'I'm sick and tired of listening to your questions,' he snarled. 'Now, for the last time, get on your horse. I won't ask you again.'

Suddenly Serape gave a cry. He had turned in his saddle and was looking up at the ridge behind them. A lone horseman had appeared, silhouetted against the skyline. The horse stood there for a moment, and then the rider urged it on down the hillside. It moved swiftly into the cover of the trees and was lost to sight.

Bandolier looked amused. 'This the big party of men you mentioned?' he said. 'They don' look like they're gonna cause much trouble.'

Alec and Coates glanced at each other, bemused. They didn't have the least idea who it might be.

They waited in silence for what seemed an eternity. Then the horseman emerged from the trees and approached at a gallop. Now Alec could see that he rode tall in the saddle, that he was broad-shouldered and wore a Stetson hat. As he came closer, Alec spotted the handle of a Colt .45 jutting from a leather holster on his right hip and a red bandana draped around his neck.

Alec had never been more pleased to see a person in his entire life.

The man drew his grey horse to a halt and sat there, looking at the two Mexicans, a confident smile on his thin lips.

'Good day, gentlemen,' said Ethan Wade. 'Looks like I got here just in time for the party.'

CHAPTER THREE

Mexican Stand-off

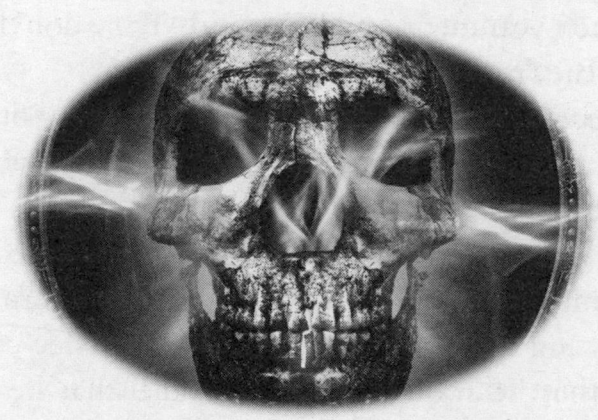

'I never thought I'd say this,' said Coates calmly, 'but I'm very pleased to see you, Mr Wade.'

'Likewise, Coates,' said Ethan, but he never took his eyes off the two Mexicans. 'I must have got to the hacienda only an hour after you left. The gardener told me where you were headed and I figured I should come straight after you. Luckily there was a spare horse.'

'Thank goodness for that,' said Coates.

'Who are you?' snapped Bandolier, but Ethan ignored him.

'I got to admit, I'm surprised at you, bringing the boy way out here,' he said.

Coates sighed. 'I can assure you, I had very little say in the matter,' he murmured. 'You know how headstrong Master Alec can be.'

'Oh yeah, he can be single-minded when he wants to be.'

'Hey, cowboy! I'm talkin' to you!' snapped Bandolier, but again Ethan acted as though he hadn't heard him.

'I'd appreciate it if you and Coates didn't talk about me as though I wasn't here,' complained Alec.

'Point taken,' said Ethan. 'You OK, kid?'

'I'm fine, thanks.'

'And who are these two *muchachos*?'

'These fine gentlemen were just inviting us to ride along with them,' explained Coates. 'One of them said something about cutting off one of Master Alec's ears and sending it to his father.'

'Is that a fact?' Ethan smiled. 'What's the matter, boys, they don't do postcards round here? Sounds downright unfriendly to me.'

Bandolier sneered. 'Who the hell do you think you are?' he asked. 'You gonna stop us from taking the boy? One man, all by himself?'

Ethan stared at him. 'I guess so,' he said. 'You got a problem with that?'

Bandolier laughed mockingly and looked across at Serape. There was a good twenty feet between them, and Serape was edging his horse sideways to make it more difficult for Ethan to cover them both.

'Oh, I see,' said Bandolier. 'You are the big tough gringo cowboy, come over here to show us how it's done, huh?'

Ethan shrugged. 'That kind of thing,' he said. 'I usually charge for lessons, but in your case I'll make an exception.'

'Well, let me point something out to you, *vaquero*. Me and my friend here, we each got a gun and we good shots. I am fast on the draw; he is even faster. You reckon you can beat both of us?'

Ethan's gaze never wavered. 'I *know* I can beat both of you,' he said. 'But me, I'm a reasonable man. I'm going to give you a chance to ride away. See, this might surprise you, but I don't like having to kill people – it kind of goes against the grain with me. Oh, I can do it and I *will* do it if I have to, but at heart I'm a peace-loving guy. I really don't want to shoot the two of you unless I absolutely have to. You see my problem?'

Bandolier laughed again, tilting back his head

to look at the sky. Alec and Coates watched the unfolding scene in tense silence.

'You're real funny,' said Bandolier at last. 'You're killing me! You talk tough too. But you know we're not going to ride away from here, don' you?'

Ethan sighed. 'I had an idea you wouldn't,' he said. 'And that saddens me. See, the way I figure it, you boys could get away clean and be in some cantina tonight, drinking mescal and telling stories about how you came real close to losing your lives, but how instead, you made the right decision. But no, you're gonna be lying in the dirt, supplying the local coyote population with supper. Heck, I know which choice I'd make.'

Bandolier stopped laughing. 'Enough of this talk!' he snapped. 'Make your move, *vaquero*.'

Ethan said nothing and made no attempt to reach for his gun. Alec watched intently, hardly daring to breathe.

'I said, make your move!'

'Oh, I'm in no hurry, *compadre*. After you.'

Bandolier's face was set in a scowl and Alec noticed that thick beads of sweat had broken out on his brow and were trickling down his face. His right arm was held out a few inches above the handle of his revolver, but Ethan's stayed by his side. The American looked relaxed, as though he had not a care in the world.

There was a long silence, broken only by the distant shrieking of a hawk.

'Hear that?' murmured Ethan. 'There's somebody else likes to dine on dead meat. Reckon he's calling all his friends to the party.'

'You talk too much,' said Bandolier.

'Well, talk is cheap and life is precious. And only a fool would throw his life away over a few pesos in ransom money.'

'I tol' you to shut up!'

'Yeah, you did. And you told me to make a move, but I haven't and neither have you. You going to use that gun? I mean, we can sit here for a few more hours if you like, but it's down to you, *amigo*.'

Bandolier's hand began to inch closer to the pistol, but now the sweat was literally pouring down his face. Suddenly he shook his head, laughing softly, and let his arm fall to his side. 'You know what,' he said. 'You're right. Why would I want to be killed? That's just stupid. A guy doesn't act like you do unless he's a real dead shot.'

'I don't like to boast,' said Ethan.

'Me and my friend, we're going to ride away now, OK?'

Ethan didn't say anything. He sat still in his saddle, watching them. Bandolier lifted his right hand well away from his gun and started to back his horse up. 'We're just going to forget we ever met,' he said. 'How does that sound to you?'

'Sounds great,' said Ethan.

Bandolier said something to Serape in Spanish. The other man looked at him, a disappointed expression on his face, but then he too took his arm away from his gun. The Mexicans turned their horses and began to ride slowly back towards the trees.

Ethan sat where he was, watching them intently. He didn't move a muscle until they were a good distance away. Then he let out a long sigh and dismounted. Alec ran over to him.

'Ethan, you were brilliant!' he yelled, clapping his hands together. 'You handled that so well. I knew you were good with a gun but I—'

He broke off when he saw the expression on Ethan's face. He looked drained, his face white and his mouth twisted into an expression of fury. His hands, where they rested against the pommel of his saddle, were shaking.

'Wh-what's wrong?' gasped Alec. 'You scared them off – they—'

'I ought to put you across my knee and paddle your backside!' snarled Ethan. 'Are you crazy? Those two came *this* close to drawing on me.' He lifted a hand, his thumb and forefinger a fraction apart. 'I could be dead now and those two *bandidos* could have taken you off to God knows where.'

'Yes, but—'

'I can't believe you and Coates came riding out here into the middle of nowhere with nobody to look after you.'

'I'll take full responsibility,' said Coates, stepping forward.

'No you won't,' Ethan told him. 'You've got to stop doing that. We both know this was Alec's idea.'

'But' – Alec pointed towards the huge stone head – 'I heard about that, and naturally I wanted to come here and see it for myself—'

'Oh, *naturally*! For Pete's sake, Alec, this is not some game you're playing.' Ethan strode past him and looked despairingly down at the picnic things. 'And this!' he exclaimed. 'Where do you think you are – at the vicarage tea party? This is

Mexico – you guys need to wake up and smell the coffee.'

'Actually, it's tea,' said Coates. 'I don't suppose you'd care for a cup?'

Ethan studied the valet with obvious irritation. 'No, I don't want a cup of tea. You English think a cup of tea will fix everything!' He turned back to look at Alec. 'You've got to start using your brains a little more,' he said. 'I always had you down as a smart kid, but you just don't think before you act!' He pointed to the distant riders, who had reached the cover of the trees. 'Those two guys could have killed me,' he said.

'But . . . you said you could beat both of them,' protested Alec.

'Yeah, I *said* that. Of course I said it! Doesn't mean I could have. They were two seasoned gun-slingers, sitting twenty feet apart . . . Who do you think I am, Billy the Kid? And can you imagine what would have happened if they *had* shot me? They were gonna cut off one of your ears, for Pete's sake.'

'Ethan, calm down,' pleaded Alec. 'Yes, I agree it was foolish of me to make this trip. And to be fair to Coates, he did his best to talk me out of it. But . . . well, I'd been cooped up in that place for weeks. I was *bored* – and you didn't turn up when you were supposed to . . .' He thought for a moment. 'Where have you been, anyway? We expected you more than a week ago.'

Ethan scowled. 'The trip over didn't go quite as smooth as I'd figured,' he said. 'The ship I came over on got stuck on a sandbank and— Hey, don't try and turn this around to be *my* fault! I got here as quick as I could – and not a minute too soon, by the look of it.' He paused to gaze at the stone head as though he'd only just noticed it. 'That *is* quite something,' he admitted. 'Aztec?'

'Olmec,' Coates corrected him. 'The first great Mexican civilization, much older than the Aztecs.'

Alec gave him an indignant look but didn't say anything.

'Yeah, well, amazing or not, I think we should be getting back to Veracruz. Just in case those boys get their courage up and come back for another try.'

'I bet you could have beaten them,' said Alec, 'if it had come to it.'

'We'll never know,' said Ethan. 'Now I suggest that we just—'

'Mr Wade!' Coates was gazing up at the skyline

beyond the trees. Ethan and Alec turned to look.

A bunch of riders had just crested the ridge — some eight or nine of them. Even at this distance, Alec could see that most of them were wearing sombreros. As he watched, Bandolier and Serape emerged from the treeline and rode up to meet them.

'Oh, that's just great,' said Ethan.

'He *said* they were with a big party,' muttered Alec. 'But I thought he was making it up, just like we were.'

Ethan said something else under his breath. He looked around and then gestured to the tethered horses. 'Mount up,' he said.

Alec frowned. 'But we can't be sure that they—'

'Mount up!' said Ethan again, striding towards his own horse. 'There must be ten men up there. If you think I'm going to try and bluff that many, you've got another think coming.'

Alec grabbed his sketchpad and stuffed it into his saddlebag before climbing up onto his horse. Meanwhile Coates was trying to cram the picnic things into the wicker hamper.

'Leave that, you idiot!' snapped Ethan. 'They're coming.'

Alec saw that this was true. The riders were spurring their mounts down the hillside, raising a cloud of dust as they did so. It wouldn't take them long to ride through the trees.

'Coates, do as you're told!' yelled Ethan.

The valet abandoned his attempts to save the picnic hamper and concentrated instead on saving his skin. He ran over to his horse and attempted to climb into the saddle. He struggled valiantly, and finally managed to haul himself up. The three of them urged their horses past the stone head and into the forested hills beyond it. Ethan led the way, his body hunched forward in the saddle as he coaxed the grey into a gallop. Alec followed close behind him, but glancing back, he saw that Coates was bouncing inexpertly up and down; it was apparent that he wasn't going to be able to keep up.

Ethan must have reached the same conclusion. He led them into the cover of the trees and Alec was obliged to duck his head for fear of being struck by overhanging branches. Ethan kept veering off the trail, through the thickest part of the forest, then cutting back. Alec surmised that he was doing his best to throw off their pursuers.

But it wasn't working. Alec glanced back and

saw that they were still being followed by as many as ten horsemen, confident riders, heads down as they rode their horses along the narrow trails. From somewhere behind came a dull crack, and something whizzed past Alec's head to career off the trunk of a tree ahead of him.

A sharp stab of fear went through him. 'They're firing at us!' he yelled, and Ethan could only glance back and nod grimly.

'Keep moving!' he shouted back and turned his horse sharply onto another trail. 'Don't give 'em an easy target!'

Alec followed suit but then noticed that they were heading down a steep grassy slope, with no cover to shield them. Just beyond that, a piece of land had been cleared of vegetation, and on that dirt strip sat something that Alec wouldn't have expected to see here in a month of Sundays. An aeroplane.

It was not like any plane he had ever seen before. For one thing, it appeared to have a corrugated metal body that shimmered in the sunlight. For another, instead of having the usual double wing, it was a monoplane. A single propeller on the plane's nose was spinning round and the engine was giving out a loud, steady roar. It was evident that it was about to take off.

Ethan immediately urged his horse towards the plane.

'What are you doing?' Alec yelled after him.

'The way Coates rides, those *bandidos* will catch us in no time!' Ethan shouted back. 'Let's see if we can't cadge a lift off these guys.'

'A lift where?' shouted Coates.

Ethan shrugged. 'Wherever the hell they're going.'

CHAPTER FOUR

A Change of Plan

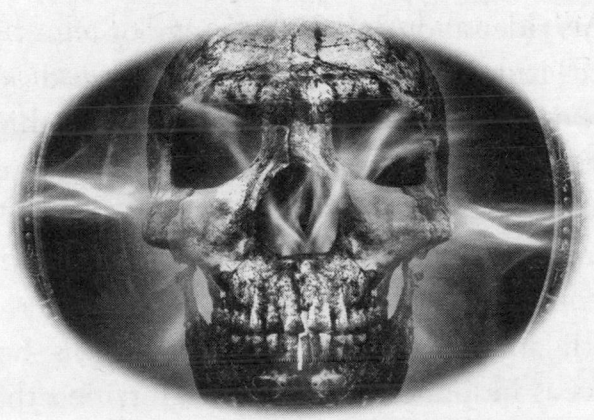

As the three friends galloped towards the plane, Alec saw to his dismay that it had begun to taxi forward. He expected Ethan to change his course but he kept riding hell for leather towards the plane, frantically waving an arm as he did so.

'We're too late!' Alec heard Coates yell from behind him; but an instant later, a door in the fuselage swung open and a red-faced man in a Panama suit leaned out, beckoning frantically to them.

Ethan urged his horse closer, and as he came alongside the open door, he leaned to the side and allowed the man to grab him around the waist, swinging him smoothly in through the opening. Ethan's horse galloped away without its rider and Alec felt a twinge of regret. That horse had been his father's pride and joy — there'd probably be hell to pay later, but this was no time to ponder the matter. Now it was his turn.

Ethan reappeared in the doorway and gestured urgently to Alec to hurry up. Alec took a deep breath and slammed his heels into his horse's flanks as he pulled it to the left, terrified that its hooves might slip on the smooth airstrip. He came alongside the opening and saw that Ethan was leaning out, the other man hanging onto his other arm to brace him. Alec glanced back and saw that the bandits were now galloping along the runway in pursuit, getting closer all the time. In that same instant, a bullet whizzed past his head, making him cringe.

'I can't do it!' he cried, but Ethan wasn't having any of that.

'You've got to,' he yelled over the roar of the engine. 'Just fall sideways — I'll catch you.'

Alec glanced back again to see Coates bouncing and flopping around in his saddle like a sack of potatoes a short distance behind him; and maybe forty yards beyond him, the bandits, closing on their prey. This was no time to hesitate. He unhooked his feet from the stirrups, snatched a deep breath and allowed himself to fall sideways in his saddle. For a heart-stopping moment he thought he had mistimed it, but Ethan's powerful arm closed around his waist and he hung there, his feet skimming inches above the ground. Then he was hauled into the plane, landing beside the red-faced man. Glancing up, he saw that there was another occupant, a sultry dark-haired young Mexican woman who was glowering down at him as though wondering where on earth he had come from. Even in the panic of the moment, Alec had time to register that she was stunningly beautiful.

But there was no time for conversation. Alec scrambled to his feet and moved to the doorway to stand beside Ethan. Together they stared out at Coates: he was trying to persuade his own mount to move closer. He looked terrified and Alec could understand why. The bandits were now only yards behind him; another shot was fired and Coates's straw sombrero went tumbling from his head.

'Come on, Coates!' bellowed Ethan. 'They're nearly upon you.'

The valet wrenched his horse sideways and administered a heavy slap to its rump, which brought it alongside the plane. He stared at Alec and Ethan helplessly for a moment – as if wondering how he had ever got into this fine mess. But he unhooked his big feet from the stirrups, released the reins and, with a wild yell, began to swing sideways. Alec grabbed his shoulder and then Ethan got an arm around his waist, but they had underestimated the weight of the big Yorkshireman and he nearly yanked them clean out of the doorway. Alec felt himself sliding, but the red-faced man grabbed hold of his belt, stopping him in his tracks. For a few terrifying moments Coates was obliged to run beside the plane, his boots dancing across the airstrip, while he unleashed a torrent of swear words the like of which Alec had never heard him use.

The closest of the bandits, a big thickset man wearing a sombrero, lifted his pistol to take aim at the struggling Coates. At such close range, it seemed unlikely that he could miss. Alec glanced wildly around the interior of the plane and his gaze fell on what looked like a rucksack hanging beside the door. Without hesitating, he scooped it up by the strap and flung it over Coates's head, straight at the bandit. It hit him full in the face, just as he was about to fire his gun; he tipped back in his saddle, flailing his arms wildly as he fell. His horse veered to one side and the riders behind him crashed into it. There was a tangle of rearing, kicking horses, and suddenly the plane was leaving them behind.

Then there was a concerted heave from all three rescuers, and Coates was lifted off the ground and in through the opening. Everyone went down in an ungainly sprawl in the cramped interior and lay there, gasping for breath.

Alec looked at the man who had just rescued him. 'I'm sorry if that was your bag,' he apologized.

The man shook his head and replied in a broad Cockney accent: 'It weren't a bag, son. It was one of the flippin' parachutes!'

There was a dull thud as a bullet punched into the fuselage and the man hurried forward and slammed the door shut; then Alec realized that somebody was shouting to him from the open cockpit. The pilot. He got onto his hands and knees and crawled through an open hatchway to see a tall, thin man grinning down at him. He was wearing a leather flying helmet and his thick goggles gave him an owlish appearance.

'Are you all right?' he yelled, with what sounded like a German accent.

Alec nodded. 'I think so,' he shouted back.

'Come on in here and grab yourself a seat, kid! Give your friends a little more room back there.' The man gestured to the co-pilot's seat. 'Strap yourself in. Why were those men chasing you?'

Alec stood up and scrambled into the spare seat. He saw now that they weren't very far from the end of the airstrip. A screen of trees and bushes barred their way. 'They wanted to cut off my ear!' he yelled back. 'They were going to take me hostage!'

'*Mein Gott.* Animals! You were lucky that Mr Campbell saw you. A few moments later and we would have been in the air.' He reached out and shook Alec's hand. 'Klaus Dorfmann,' he cried. 'At your service.'

Alec nodded. 'Aren't we a bit close to the end of the runway?' he asked nervously.

Klaus nodded. 'I was just thinking the same

thing. I'm afraid we're going to have to turn the plane round.'

Alec stared at him. 'You're kidding!'

'I never kid,' Klaus assured him, his voice calm, matter-of-fact. Then he stamped a foot down on a pedal at his feet, yanked on a brake, and magically, the plane's nose began to come round.

'How are you doing that?' shouted Alec. 'I thought we'd all have to get out and push!'

Klaus laughed. 'Ah, but you're thinking of biplanes. This is a Junkers F13. This machine can do things you've only dreamed of.'

Alec saw that the bandits had now recovered from their collision and were urging their horses forward again, galloping straight towards the oncoming plane. 'What happens now?' he cried.

Klaus didn't seem in the least bit perturbed. 'We get to play a little game,' he said. 'I think the Americans like to call it "Chicken".' He glanced over his shoulder. 'Everyone OK back there?' A chorus of muffled shouts came from the cabin. 'Good. Now, I think we've hung around long enough . . .' The pilot coaxed the power up again and the plane lunged forward as though it had been straining at an invisible leash. It went speed-ing towards the Mexicans.

Alec stared down the runway in horrified fascination. The bandits were approaching rapidly – much too quickly for comfort. Then Bandolier, who was in the lead, raised his gun and Alec saw a puff of smoke emerge from the barrel. An instant later, there was a dull thud as the bullet glanced off the fuselage just above his head, but Klaus didn't slow down. Now Alec could see the looks of panic on the bandits' dirty faces as the plane came roaring towards them. He steeled himself for the terrible impact when the plane's propeller ploughed into them . . . But at the last moment, they pulled their horses aside. Then the plane was hurtling past them and lifting off. It rose steadily, but more trees were approaching and Alec pictured the plane smashing into them and exploding on impact . . .

'Come on!' yelled Klaus to nobody in particular. And then he added something in German, which Alec didn't understand.

The wheels tore chunks of foliage from the topmost branches of the trees, but the plane kept rising and then suddenly they were clear and all the dangers were left behind. Alec gave a shout of exaltation, but the wind sweeping through the open cockpit snatched his breath away. The plane banked hard and came racing back over the runway. Alec could see the horsemen far below, already dwarfed into miniature, firing their guns upwards in a last desperate attempt to halt the plane, but they might as well have been firing peashooters.

'You did it!' cried Alec. 'You saved our necks!'

'*Ja.*' Klaus grinned. He turned to look at Alec. 'Now tell me,' he said. 'What were the three of you doing out there in the middle of nowhere?'

Back in the cabin, Ethan and Coates were thanking the man who had just saved their lives. His name, it transpired, was Frank Campbell, and he was a Londoner.

Ethan shook his hand warmly. 'I figure we're in your debt,' he said, shouting above the roar of the engines. 'Those men would have shot us down like dogs.'

'It's a bloomin' miracle I saw you,' Frank yelled back as they settled themselves into the leather seats in the cramped interior. 'I just happened to glance out of the window and I said to Conchita, "Blimey, there's some blokes gallopin' towards us and it looks like they're in trouble." Then I shouted to Herr Dorfmann to slow down a bit.'

Ethan raised his eyebrows. 'Herr Dorfmann?'

'The pilot, Klaus. He's a German.'

Coates scowled. 'Well, we won't hold it against him,' he muttered. 'I suppose the war's been over five years now. Time to forgive and forget.'

'That's big of you considering he just saved our necks,' laughed Ethan.

The Mexican woman, Conchita, was sitting staring sullenly at the newcomers. She didn't seem as friendly as Frank. 'How do we know these men aren't *bandidos*?' she snapped. 'They must have done something real bad to be chased like that.'

Coates shook his head. 'I can assure you, madam, *they* were the perpetrators,' he told her. 'We were merely trying to enjoy a quiet picnic when they approached us and started making overtures of an unsavoury nature.'

Conchita looked at Frank. 'What he saying?' she snarled. 'He talk funny.'

'Oh, that's all right, Conchita, I think the gentleman's just from the north – ain't that right, Mr . . . ?'

'Coates. And this is Mr Ethan Wade. And the young gentleman in the cockpit is Master Devlin, for whom I valet.'

Conchita looked mystified by this. 'You a servant?' she asked.

Coates forced a smile. 'I prefer the word valet,' he insisted.

The plane hit an air pocket and shuddered violently. Coates looked around nervously, but refrained from saying anything.

'So what was the plane doing out here in the middle of nowhere?' shouted Ethan. 'Don't think I'm complaining or anything, but . . . it was the last thing I expected to see.'

Frank nodded. 'I hired Herr Dorfmann to take us across to the south coast,' he said. 'He works cheap and doesn't like to pay for space at airports. This was the only strip he could pick us up from. I must confess, I was nervous about it being such a remote spot and everything. But we reckoned it was worth takin' the risk. This is the opportunity of a lifetime.' He smiled at Conchita with evident pride. 'You see, I'm taking Conchita to Tonala for a screen test.'

'Oh yeah?' Ethan looked at him blankly. 'What's that?'

Conchita glared at him. 'Don' you know what a screen test is?' she cried. 'It's what they give you when you're gonna be a movie star.'

'Hey, you're putting me on!'

Frank shook his head. 'On the level, Mr Wade. And it's not just any old run-of-the-mill screen test, neither. It's with Louis B. Mayer, just about the biggest name in the motion picture business.'

Ethan must have looked puzzled, so Frank continued, 'You know: *The Woman He Married*? *He Who Gets Slapped*?'

Ethan nodded. He hadn't heard of the films, but didn't like to say so. 'And, er . . . what's a big-shot motion picture producer doing in a dump like Tonala?' he asked.

'Is not a dump!' snapped Conchita. 'Is very nice town. My cousin live there.'

Frank smiled. 'Mr Louis B. Mayer's shooting a movie in Tonala. A Latin romance, I believe. I sent him a telegraph telling him all about Conchita and he's agreed to give her a screen test.'

'How wonderful,' said Coates tonelessly. 'And what exactly does it entail?'

'A little bit of acting,' said Conchita. 'But mostly, just looking beautiful.'

'I've told Mr Mayer all about her stunnin' Latin looks,' said Frank.

'Hmm. And did you mention her natural

modesty?' asked Coates, without raising an eyebrow.

'I mentioned everything,' said Frank, missing the dig entirely. 'Cost me a small fortune, it did, to put it all in a telegram, but it seems to have done the trick. Let's face it, when he gets a look at Conchita, he can't fail to sign her up.'

'I don't get to see many moving pictures,' said Ethan. 'Never seem to be in a place that has a nickelodeon.'

Frank chuckled. 'Forgive me, Mr Wade, but they've come on a bit since the days of the nickelodeons. Now they have real stories and most pictures last for over an hour.'

'Over an hour?' Ethan stared at Frank. 'Who would want to sit and watch a screen for that long?'

'Anybody would if Conchita was up there,' said Frank, and he smiled adoringly at the back of the would-be star's head.

Ethan smiled. Conchita *was* pretty in a moody, Latin sort of way, but unfortunately she seemed to have the disposition of a rattlesnake with a belly ache. It was evident to Ethan that Frank was mad about her and was using their professional relationship as an excuse to be with her. Ethan was intrigued.

'So how did you two hook up?' he asked.

Frank looked slightly bashful. 'Well, my background is in music hall. I used to work for Fred Karno at the Fun Factory in Camberwell . . .'

Ethan didn't have a clue what Frank was talking about, but Coates seemed to be familiar with the name.

'Mr Karno is, I believe, the impresario who discovered Charlie Chaplin,' he said. 'Before he became a star of moving pictures himself.'

Now Ethan was impressed. 'Charlie Chaplin,' he said. 'Wow! I don't go to the moving pictures, but I've heard of *him*!'

'Oh yes, he was one of our acts,' said Frank proudly. 'Officially I was Fred's associate producer, but I wasn't much more than a glorified errand boy. I wanted to find acts of me own. Anyhow, I came out to Acapulco for a holiday and I happened to see Conchita in the chorus line of this musical revue, *One Night in Acapulco*. Well, it was obvious to me that she was destined for bigger things – know what I mean? So I offered to manage her career.'

Conchita leaned forward as if to confide a secret. 'Frank say to me, I can be bigger than Mary Pickford.'

Ethan tried not to laugh. He somehow couldn't see Conchita taking the place of the young actress who was currently known as 'America's sweetheart', but then he would be the first to admit that he knew nothing about this new industry — and who could have predicted that a shy young boy from one of the poorest slums in London would go on to become a star of the magnitude of Charlie Chaplin?

'Yeah, but Conchita's more your mysterious type — dark, moody. I've got these plans for a series of pictures featuring Conchita Velez, the Mexican Wildcat.'

Ethan didn't quite know what to say to that. Coates, on the other hand, didn't mind voicing his opinions.

'I can't help feeling that Miss Velez would be advised to set her sights a little lower to start with. Maybe begin with smaller roles. It would be a shame to aim too high and come a cropper.'

'What you know?' snarled Conchita, glaring down at him. 'You just a servant anyway.'

Coates opened his mouth to reply, but then the engine started to whine and the plane began to descend. He looked alarmed but Frank patted his shoulder reassuringly.

'Don't worry, Mr Coates. We're just makin' a quick stop before we set off across the rainforest. Gotta pick up another passenger at the oil fields.'

'Ah.' Coates nodded in evident relief. 'You must forgive me but there's something about planes that makes me nervous.'

'No need for that,' Frank assured him. 'Herr Dorfmann tells me this plane is the finest in all Mexico. He's flown coast to coast dozens of times without a problem.'

Coates smiled thinly. 'I'm glad to hear it,' he said. 'Master Alec was involved in a flight in Egypt last year.' He glanced accusingly at Ethan. 'It didn't end well.'

Ethan made a dismissive gesture. 'Heck, Coates, that was different. For one thing, I'd never flown that kind of plane before – and for another, we were being attacked by hundreds of bats . . .' He noticed Frank staring at him in alarm and changed the subject. 'So,' he said, 'er . . . where exactly are we stopping off?'

CHAPTER FIVE

Desperate Measures

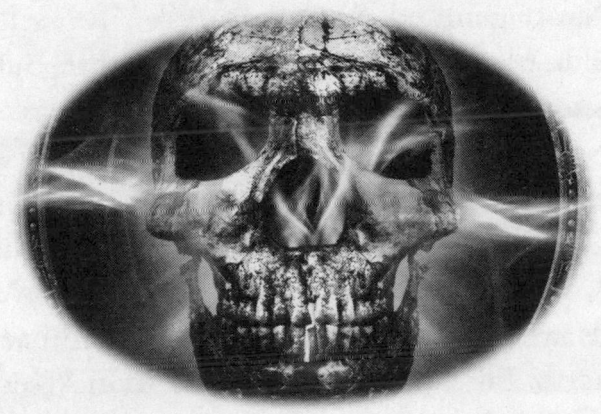

Klaus eased the plane down expertly and landed on an airstrip behind a high wire fence. In the distance Alec could see the tall shapes of metal oil derricks.

Klaus brought the plane to a halt, then removed his goggles and flying helmet and gestured to Alec. 'Come on,' he said. 'Let's go and meet our new passenger.' He climbed out of the cockpit and down some metal rungs to the ground. Alec followed him round to the rear of the plane. The cabin door opened and the other passengers emerged, grateful for the chance to stretch their legs.

Ethan hurried straight over to Klaus and shook his hand. 'Thanks a million,' he said. 'We owe you our lives.'

Klaus grinned. 'My pleasure,' he said. 'I wouldn't leave anybody in a fix like that. But . . . er, listen, I'm afraid I'm going to have to ask you for some money. I *am* trying to run a business here.'

'Of course,' muttered Coates. 'You will be paid, sir, I can assure you of that. We have no funds with us, but just as soon as we're back in Veracruz I'll arrange to have the money sent to you.' He glanced around. 'So . . . these are the famous Veracruz oilfields?'

Klaus nodded. 'The last stop before the Huasteca Veracruzana,' he said.

'What's that?' asked Alec.

'The tropical rainforest,' said Klaus airily. 'We'll be flying across it en route to Tonala. The question is – what are we going to do with you? There's really only room for four passengers in the back and one in the front, which means we're going to be short of a seat.'

'Short of *two* seats, I reckon,' said Frank, pointing.

Everyone turned to look. Two men were

approaching the plane, both of them carrying bags. Oddly they were not walking side by side, but several yards apart, as though the second man was following the first.

The leader was tall and distinguished looking, dressed in a pearl-grey suit and a checked shirt. As he drew closer they could hear him speaking in an American accent.

'Say, what's going on? There seem to be more people on this plane than I figured.'

Klaus nodded. 'An unexpected event, Mr Nelson,' he said. 'These three people were being chased by bandits – I couldn't leave them to their fate.'

Nelson seemed to consider this for a moment. Ethan took the initiative and stepped forward to offer his hand.

'Ethan Wade,' he said. 'This here is Alec Devlin and the guy who looks like he just swallowed a sour apple is called Coates.'

The tall man nodded and grinned, showing even white teeth. He took the hand and shook it vigorously. 'I'm Ulysses T. Nelson,' he announced grandly, as though Ethan should have heard of him. 'Oil man. Always good to meet a fellow American.'

Behind him, the second passenger smiled sarcastically at this. He was small and dark, with shoulder-length black hair and a ragged beard. He was dressed in a sweat-stained khaki shirt and trousers, with a battered slouch hat pulled down over his eyes. A Mexican, Alec decided, and when he spoke his accent confirmed it.

'Relax, Mr Nelson,' he said. 'Unlikely as it may seem, I don't think he has heard of you.'

Nelson's lip curled into a sneer. 'I didn't suppose for one moment that he had,' he said, without turning round. 'You'll have to excuse him . . .' He jerked a thumb over his shoulder. 'That's Luis Chavez. My shadow. He follows me everywhere.'

'Why's that?' asked Ethan.

'Oh, believe me, it wasn't my idea. But Luis works with this so-called environmentalist group, the Huasteca Alliance. The government seems to think it's a good idea if he checks out how things work in my organization. I'm obliged to give him access. I didn't figure on him flying with me to Tonala though. May I enquire why these villains were after you, Mr Wade?'

'They were planning to kidnap young Alec

here and hold him to ransom. His father's with the British embassy in Veracruz.'

Nelson shook his head. 'There are some nasty characters around,' he admitted. 'Everyone says the revolution's over but nobody seems to have told the Mexicans.'

Coates looked at Alec triumphantly. 'Didn't I tell you the very same thing, Master Alec?' he said. 'But would you listen to me? Oh no.'

Klaus looked doubtfully at Luis Chavez. 'Were you planning to come with us too?' he said. 'Ordinarily, there would be a spare seat, but—'

'I have money,' said Luis; and he took a large bundle of grimy-looking dollar bills out of his pocket. 'I can pay you.'

Nelson raised his eyebrows. 'Hey, that's a lot of dough, Luis. What did you do, rob a bank?' He laughed unpleasantly.

'I've been saving up,' Luis told him. 'And I have to be in Tonala by tomorrow. An urgent appointment.' He looked at Klaus. 'You wouldn't leave me behind, would you?'

Klaus frowned. 'Well, I could certainly use the extra money,' he admitted. 'Business has been slow lately.' He looked at Nelson. 'Perhaps I could leave these three people here and pick them up on my way back through?'

But Nelson shook his head. 'Out of the question,' he said. 'Only official personnel allowed on my oilfield.' He glanced at Luis. 'And those with government clearance. It's a dangerous place.'

'It is *your* oilfield?' cried Conchita. 'You must be a very rich man!'

Nelson smiled. 'I do all right for myself, Miss—'

'Velez,' interrupted Frank. 'Conchita Velez. A motion picture star of tomorrow. I'm taking her to Tonala for a screen test with Louis B. Mayer.'

'Gosh,' said Alec. 'He's famous!'

Coates looked at him. 'You've heard of him?' he asked.

'Of course. *The Woman He Married*? *He Who Gets Slapped*?'

Frank grinned. 'Yeah, see – there's a kid who reads his *Picturegoer* magazine!'

Alec grinned. 'When I can track down a copy,' he said. 'It's hard to find in Veracruz.'

Klaus was looking from the plane to the passengers and back again, as though weighing them up. 'So there's no way these people can stay on the site?' he asked.

'No way,' said Nelson. 'I'm sorry, Herr Dorfmann, but I have rules and I never break them.'

'What's the matter?' asked Luis slyly. 'Afraid they might see something they don't approve of?'

'Of course not!' Nelson told the others, nodding at the Mexican. 'Ignore him. I have to let *him* visit, but believe me, if I had my way . . .' He left the sentence unfinished and looked doubtfully at the plane. 'Think that old crate can carry eight people?' he muttered.

Klaus looked insulted by the question. 'Mr Nelson, this is a Junkers F13! Of course it can carry eight, no problem. True, only six of us will have seats — the other two will have to sit on the floor between the rows. It won't be very comfortable but I can take you to Tonala and then back to Veracruz the day after tomorrow. As a gesture, I will reduce your fares by ten per cent.'

'You're all heart,' observed Coates.

'Say, I haven't been in Tonala for years,' said Ethan wistfully. 'Used to be a little bar there where they served the best tequila cocktails in Mexico. There was a pretty little waitress too, name of Maria. I was sweet on her for a while . . .'

'I thought you said it is a dump?' said Conchita.

'Well . . . maybe I was being a little hard on it. I had good times there.'

'Fascinating though this is,' said Coates, 'there's a more pressing problem. Will we be able to get a message to Master Alec's father to let him know everything's all right?'

Ethan nodded. 'Oh sure, I seem to remember there's a telegraph office in the main square – isn't that right, Miss Velez?'

Conchita gave a surly nod. 'Sure they have one,' she replied. 'Tonala is very modern town.'

'Well, that's settled then,' said Klaus. He looked at Alec. 'You'll come with us to Tonala. You may as well stay in the co-pilot's seat. Actually, it's quite something flying over the Huasteca. Very few planes cross it. There are parts of it where no white man has ever walked.'

'Gosh,' said Alec. 'And . . . the plane will carry us all safely?'

'Of course.' Klaus patted the silver flank of his plane as though it were a favourite horse. 'This is the most advanced monoplane in the world,' he said proudly. 'It cost me a small fortune, which is why I will be working for years to pay back the loan. But what you are looking at here is the future of civil aviation. Soon these planes will be carrying passengers to every destination in the world.'

'Very nice, I'm sure,' said Coates. 'But before we set off, can I just ask . . . ?' He leaned forward to whisper something to the pilot.

Klaus laughed in disbelief. 'No, it doesn't have a water closet!' He pointed to a screen of bushes beside the airstrip. 'You'd better go behind there,' he said, and Coates walked quickly away, his face reddening. The German looked around at the others. 'And if anybody else needs to pay a visit before we set off, you should take the oppor-tunity now. It's a long time before we touch down again.'

There was a moment of indecision and then Alec, Ethan and Frank all turned as one and hurried after Coates. Klaus looked at Conchita, but she gave him a glare. He turned and went back to the cockpit.

'I'll just make a few last-minute checks,' he said.

Sitting in the co-pilot's seat, Alec felt the back of his seat pushing against his spine as the plane took off and rose swiftly into the air. Below, he saw an extraordinary sight: rows of tall steel derricks and, around them, men milling about like industrious ants. There were huts and sheds and what looked like garages for the automobiles; and then a huge pool of black fluid. Even up here, high above it all, the smell of it hung heavy in the air.

'That little landing strip is only temporary, by the way,' shouted Nelson through the open doorway. 'I already have plans to extend it.'

Luis Chavez snorted derisively. 'Oh yes, the rich Yankee with the big plans! What Señor Nelson omits to point out is that those oil wells are standing on what was once several hundred acres of tropical rainforest. And in order to drill those wells he has cut down thousands of trees.'

Nelson made a dismissive gesture. 'I don't know why Señor Chavez is on my case all the time. Anyone would think he doesn't want his country to make progress.'

'You call that progress?' snapped Luis. 'You people have been in Veracruz more than fifteen years and I don't see any progress. I see the destruction of one of the country's natural resources – pollution on an incredible scale . . .

And let's not forget about the tribes that live in the rainforest, the people you are making homeless.'

Alec looked down. More of the lakes of crude oil were appearing now, like great black tumours on the earth. From up here they appeared small but he knew that some of them must hold thousands of gallons. More and more of them appeared, interspersed with derricks, machinery and dilapidated buildings.

Nelson was appealing to the others in the cabin now and Alec turned back to listen, ducking his head through the doorway. Sitting opposite the oil man, Conchita looked fascinated, but Alec suspected that it was Nelson's wealth that had got her attention. In the seat immediately behind her, Frank was clearly worried that she might be a bit too interested in the American. Coates and Ethan were sitting cross-legged on the floor, jammed into the narrow gap between the seats. Coates was studying Nelson as he might an insect that had just crawled out of a half-eaten crumpet; Ethan's face betrayed no emotion whatsoever.

'Señor Chavez here seems to have made it his mission in life to follow me around,' complained

Nelson. 'Everywhere I go, there he is at my side, nagging about how I'm despoiling his beautiful country. He's a naturalist, apparently. At least that's what he calls himself. "Troublemaker" would be a more accurate description. He doesn't seem to appreciate that I have made millions for these people.'

'You've made millions for yourself, you mean!' said Luis.

'You're a millionaire?' gasped Conchita. 'Ay-yi!'

'Yes, he is,' Luis told her. 'But I don't see a lot of Mexicans making much. Oh, the landowners, they get paid a reasonable amount, but nothing like what their land is worth. And those who won't sell . . . well, they seem to suffer terrible accidents. Anyone who stands in the way of this . . . progress, they get cut down, just like the rainforest.'

'I'm warning you,' snarled Nelson. 'Don't make allegations you cannot back up.'

Luis shrugged his narrow shoulders. 'OK, let's talk about things I don't need to prove,' he said. 'Things that are common knowledge. What about the fact that Mexicans can only hold menial jobs in your organization?'

Conchita's expression was suddenly rather less friendly. 'This is true?' she asked.

'Well, he's just twisting things—'

'It's undeniable,' persisted Luis. 'Let's also talk about the "whites-only" social clubs you've set up – and the stinking slums you allow your native workers to live in. And oh, let's talk about Dos Bocas, shall we?'

Nelson flinched. 'Well,' he said, 'of course that was unfortunate. But in all industries there are accidents – that's just part of the process.'

'What's Dos Bocas?' asked Ethan.

'It's a place that used to be called San Diego del Mar,' said Luis. 'A beautiful area of lakes and jungle. Fifteen years ago an oil well exploded—'

'Not one of mine,' said Nelson hastily.

'No, not one of his,' admitted Luis. 'But somebody very like him. The fire burned for over fifty days. They tried every way they knew to snuff it out, but they could not. When it finally burned itself out, they found it had spilled four hundred and twenty million gallons of crude oil over thirty square miles. Now there is a lake so poisonous that nothing can live in it – and scientists believe that in a hundred years' time it will still be the same.'

'That's terrible,' shouted Alec, over the bluster of the wind.

'I agree it's a shame,' said Nelson. 'But, you see, that's what happens when people try to cut corners. That's not the way we do it. We always observe proper safety procedures.'

'Is that right?' said Luis. 'I wonder if the thirty-four employees who have died or been injured this year alone would agree with you.'

'Thirty-four?' echoed Frank. 'That don't sound too healthy.'

'You see what he does?' said Nelson. 'Always emphasizing the negative. There are thousands of automobiles driving around this country because of my wells.'

'I don't own an automobile,' said Luis. 'And this may surprise you, Señor Nelson, but neither do many of my countrymen.'

'Yeah, well, only because you're so stubborn. Didn't I offer to give you a Ford only last month?'

'You tried to buy me off,' said Luis. 'But I didn't want your bribe.'

'You offered him an automobile?' Conchita suddenly seemed impressed again.

'I just figured if he was going to spend so

much time following me around, I should make life a little easier for him.'

'I would *love* an automobile,' sighed Conchita. 'A big one.'

'And you will have it, my dear,' Frank assured her. 'Just as soon as we sign that contract with Mr Louis B. Mayer.'

'That's how Señor Nelson does business, I guess,' said Luis. 'He buys people off. But the one thing I do want, he cannot give me.'

'Which is . . . ?' grunted Nelson.

'All those thousands of acres returned. In their original condition.'

'Yes, well, now you're just being ridiculous! You know perfectly well that's not possible.'

Klaus tapped Alec on the shoulder, pointing down. Alec saw that they were finally leaving the last of the oil industry behind. The rainforest rose up suddenly, dense, mysterious, seemingly impenetrable – but he could see that machinery was already at work, cutting down more of it.

'We're heading out over the jungle now!' he shouted into the cabin.

Luis gave a sad smile. 'Take a good long look at it, kid,' he said, 'while you still can. I guarantee, in fifty years it will all be gone.'

'But . . . it's *huge*,' said Alec. 'Surely they can't take it all?'

Everybody looked at Nelson, as if expecting him to give an answer, but he said nothing. Everyone stopped talking and there was just the roar of the engine as the plane sped onwards towards its destination.

CHAPTER SIX

Snake in the Grass

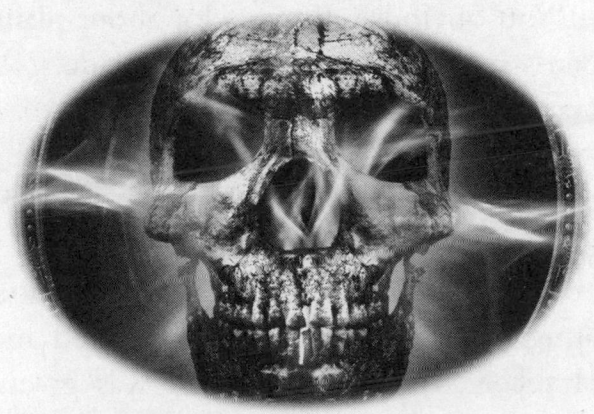

They flew for hours over the great stretch of rainforest and Alec found himself wondering if Luis Chavez had been exaggerating. How could so much jungle disappear in such a short space of time? When he looked down, he saw nothing breaking up the dense green depths but the occasional river, coiling and twisting like a giant serpent.

'It's quite something, isn't it?' yelled Klaus, over the noise of the engine.

Alec glanced up, surprised. 'Yes,' he shouted back. 'It's magnificent.'

Klaus studied the boy for a moment. 'You

have been in a plane before, I think.'

'Just once,' admitted Alec. 'In Egypt.' But he didn't want to dwell on what had happened there. 'You obviously know a lot about planes.'

Klaus nodded with evident pride. 'I was decorated,' he said. 'In the Great War.'

'Really? Ethan flew planes in the war,' said Alec. 'Hey, who knows? Perhaps the two of you were in a dogfight with each other!'

'I doubt it,' said Klaus. 'I had a reputation for shooting down everyone who attacked me. In fact I received several medals. I was given the *Pour la Mérite*, the ultimate award for a pilot. It was presented to me by none other than Manfred von Richthofen. You have heard of the Red Baron, *ja*?'

Alec nodded. 'Oh yes – he was famous, wasn't he?'

'A brilliant pilot and a great personal friend of mine. When he was shot down and killed in nineteen eighteen, he had over eighty Allied planes to his credit.' The German suddenly looked embarrassed. 'But I don't suppose you want to hear about that.'

Alec shrugged. 'It's all history now,' he said. 'I was only ten years old when the war ended. My father was a diplomat – he wasn't called up – so it didn't really affect me that much. I don't understand why people can't just get on together . . . You know,' he went on, 'your English is very good.'

'Thank you. Well, yes, I went to college in England before the war. I was in Manchester studying engineering. I would have been a good engineer, I think. But then of course, the war intervened.' Klaus smiled sadly. 'There is still, I think, a lot of resentment towards the Germans because of the war. People don't say much, but the man with you – not the American, the other one . . .'

'Coates?'

'Yes. He gave me a certain look when he heard my accent. I get this often. But you have to understand, I was just doing my duty. I was called up like everybody else. I always knew I didn't want to be stuck on the ground with the infantry, so I enrolled in the Luftstreitkräfte – the German Army Air Service.' He scowled. 'After the war, the service was dissolved, all our planes destroyed – and former air force pilots were forbidden to fly anything other than kites. I knew that if I wanted to continue to fly, I would have to leave the country.'

'So how did you end up in Mexico?'

'I came here four years ago when they founded the Mexican air force. They needed instructors. I worked for them for a year, but the conditions were terrible. I quickly realized this country was going to need some civil aviation and that's when I decided to set myself up in business. Luckily I had saved enough money to put down a deposit on this plane. Now I fly passengers, mail, cargo – anything that pays my wages. It's varied work, I suppose.'

Alec studied Klaus's thin face for a moment, noting the sour look. 'But you miss the war?' he asked.

The pilot shrugged. 'I miss the excitement . . . the action. When I flew missions, I never knew if I was going to come back alive. I think for anyone who experienced those times, everything else is going to seem . . . tame.'

Alec looked down at the incredible landscape below and wondered how anybody could possibly find such an awe-inspiring sight tame, but he thought he understood. If he was honest with himself, his life since the adventures of the previous summer had seemed somewhat mundane. Even the excitement of coming to a new country had been short-lived – especially once he had been introduced to Señor Vargas.

'Well, I suppose it's not all humdrum,' he argued. 'We *were* being shot at by bandits only a couple of hours back.'

Klaus forced a smile. 'Yes, that at least was out of the ordinary,' he admitted. 'And I suppose this is a lot better than sitting at an office desk every day. Hey – look!'

Klaus pointed away to his left and Alec turned his head. A huge eagle was soaring on the warm thermal currents, coasting alongside the plane as though trying to keep pace with it; but the Junkers engine proved too powerful, and after a few minutes they left it behind.

Back in the cabin, Frank was talking about Conchita Velez and how wonderful she was. The way he saw it, she was going to be the biggest movie sensation of the decade.

'Just wait until she gets in front of that camera,' he said. 'She's gonna knock 'em dead!'

Ethan smiled politely, but wondered once again if Frank wasn't kidding himself. Good looks were one thing – Conchita had no problems on that score; but if the movie cameras picked up even half of that moodiness, viewers would never come to see her onscreen again. However, it soon became apparent that she had impressed at least one other person.

'Miss Velez,' said Ulysses T. Nelson, leaning across the narrow aisle as if to confide something, 'I'm going to be in Tonala for a few days. I'm looking at some potential land investments just outside of the town. I'd be honoured if you'd have dinner with me one evening.'

Conchita fluttered her eyelashes. 'Oh, well, I don' know about that,' she said.

'Did I mention I have contacts in the moving picture business? Out in California there's this little place in the hills called Hollywoodland. Everyone says it's going to be the centre of the motion picture industry in years to come. I also know a few people at the Universal Film Manufacturing Company. I'm sure I could put in a good word for you.'

Conchita's dark eyes seemed to increase in size, while just behind her, Frank's round red face couldn't conceal a look of dismay.

'Maybe we *could* meet up,' she said.

'There's no need. We'll be signin' with Mr

Louis B. Mayer — you can depend on it,' Frank assured her.

'Of course,' said Nelson smoothly. 'But if for any reason things don't work out with him, I'll be staying at the Hotel Lazaro. You can always leave a message for me at the desk.' He sat back in his seat, looking pleased with himself.

Behind him, Luis rolled his eyes. He had just pulled out a large pocket watch and was studying it intently. 'You see, Señor Campbell, that's how Señor Nelson operates,' he said. 'It's amazing how easily impressed some people are by promises. And who knows, maybe he does have contacts in the moving picture business — or maybe he just wants a little company during his stay in Tonala.'

'I've had just about enough of you, Chavez,' growled Nelson, looking over his shoulder. 'Why don't you keep your nose out of things that don't concern you?'

'Yes,' said Conchita. 'This is no business of yours!'

Luis laughed bitterly. 'I just don' like to see anyone being deceived,' he said. 'But you are right of course. I should stick to my own plans.' He put his watch back into his pocket. 'And it's time to get things moving.'

'What things, exactly?' asked the oil man. 'I don't know, Luis . . . I turn up at the landing strip today and there's you, waiting for the same plane. I know you like to follow me around, but this is getting ridiculous! People are starting to talk. What kind of business could you possibly have in Tonala?'

Luis shook his head. 'I don' have no business there, Señor Nelson. I'm not even planning to go to Tonala.' He picked up his bag and rummaged around inside it.

'What are you talking about? What do you mean, you're not planning to go there? That's where we're headed, isn't it?'

When Luis's hand emerged from his bag, it was holding a pistol. He thrust the barrel against the back of Nelson's head. Conchita gave a gasp of terror and shrank back against the window, as if trying to put as much distance as she could between herself and the gun.

'None of us are going to Tonala, Señor Nelson,' said the Mexican. 'Not just yet. There will be a small change of plan.' With his free hand he pulled out a sheet of paper, which he held out to Ethan. 'Take the paper, Mr Wade . . . Real careful now.'

Ethan did as he was told. He saw that it was a set of hand-written instructions.

'I want you to give that to the pilot,' said Luis calmly. 'Tell him to change course. I don' want nobody to worry. We will make a little detour, that's all. Señor Nelson will be getting off with me, and then your plane will be refuelled and the rest of you can go on your way. Tell Señor Dorfmann, if he doesn't do what I ask, I will start shooting.'

Ethan gazed scornfully at him. 'Don't do this,' he said. 'This isn't your style.'

Luis laughed. 'What are you talking about? You don' even know me.'

'I know enough to appreciate that this isn't the kind of move that comes easy to a man like you. You've got to try and achieve change the right way.'

'I *have* tried,' Luis told him. 'Everything I can think of. I've tried reasoning with this man, I've tried pleading with him, but he never listens.' A look of rage came into his dark eyes. 'Two months ago, I and the other members of the Huasteca Alliance contacted Señor Nelson. We told him about a native village that lay in the path of his forest clearance. He assured us that they would be left unharmed. A week ago I went to visit that village . . .' Now his eyes filled with tears. 'It was gone, the huts destroyed, the people dead. Eventually I found one frightened child hiding in the forest. He told me that white men had come in the night and set fire to the huts, then started killing the villagers as they tried to run—'

'I hope you're not suggesting I had anything to do with that!' protested Nelson indignantly. 'I never went near any village.'

'Oh, not you,' admitted Luis. 'People like you don't do their own dirty work. You hire others to do it for you.' He raised his left arm and dashed away the tears with his shirtsleeve. 'So now I finish trying to persuade you nicely. Now I take you hostage and we see if other people listen to what I have to say.'

'This is nuts,' said Nelson, gazing straight ahead. 'You haven't thought this through, Chavez. They won't give you a plugged nickel.'

'Oh, but I don' want money. That's the last thing I want! I have friends waiting at a landing strip in the jungle – somewhere they'll never find us. People who think like I do.'

'Terrorists, you mean.'

'No. Other members of the Huasteca Alliance. People who have realized we're not getting anywhere trying to do this through official channels. People who are prepared to do anything necessary to protect the rainforest. We'll put the plane down there and we'll get a message to your people in Veracruz: "Cut back on land clearance or we'll send you your boss's head." Then maybe we'll see some action.'

'Young man,' said Coates calmly, 'I understand you have grievances with Mr Nelson, but believe me, this is not the way to settle them.'

'Thanks for the advice,' said Luis. 'But you didn't see that village. You didn't see what his people did to helpless women and children.' He glanced around at the others. 'I'm sorry,' he said, 'but the rest of you will have to wait for a while. It will not take too long, and then you can go on your way. Miss Velez, I hope you will be in Tonala for your appointment.' He nodded at Ethan. 'Take the message, *vaquero*,' he said. 'Now.'

Ethan frowned and nodded. He got slowly to his feet and headed towards the cockpit; and at that instant, Frank Campbell threw himself across the aisle at Luis, grabbing his gun arm and wrenching it sideways. There was the sharp crack of the gun firing, the bullet missing Nelson's head by inches and punching right through the aluminium partition between cockpit and cabin. Frank started wrestling with Luis, and Coates scrambled up to lend him a hand. Ethan was about to turn back and help them but he froze as he heard Alec give a yell of terror from the cockpit. The plane suddenly pitched forward and Ethan had to fling out his arms to stop himself falling.

There was a moment when time seemed to slow down. Ethan stood there, clinging to the arm of a seat and looking at the chaos in front of him. Coates and Frank were still struggling with Luis. Nelson was slumped in his seat, his hands held to his ears after being almost deafened by the pistol shot. Conchita was backed up against the cabin window, screaming in terror. Then Ethan realized that the plane was losing height at a terrifying rate. He swore under his breath and half staggered, half fell towards the cockpit. Alec was sitting in the co-pilot's seat in silent terror. Beside him, Klaus was slumped over the controls, blood pumping from a bullet wound in his back.

CHAPTER SEVEN

The Descent

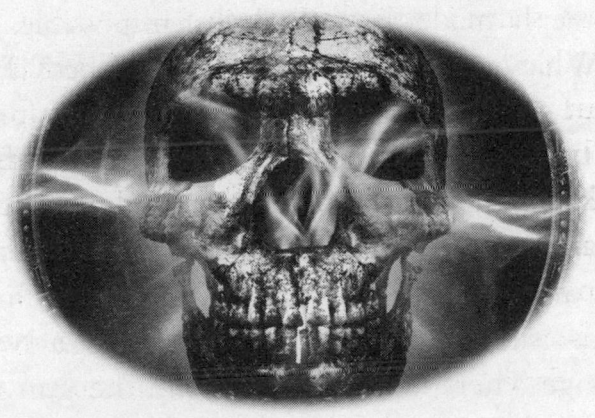

To Alec everything seemed to have been plunged, quite suddenly, into madness. One moment he'd been sitting there without a care in the world, enjoying the sensation of flying and gazing down at the lush green landscape unfolding far below him. The next, the bullet had punched through the back of Klaus's seat and slammed into his spine, flinging him forward over the controls. Instantly, the plane's nose had dropped, and once again Alec was experiencing that sickening sensation of falling helplessly out of the sky.

Then Ethan burst through the doorway and

started to try and prise Klaus away from the controls, but it was horribly cramped in the cockpit, and the fact that they were descending so steeply made the task almost impossible.

'What is it with you and aeroplanes?' Ethan yelled at Alec as he tried to get his hands on the joystick. 'Remind me not to let you get in one ever again.'

'What happened?' gasped Alec. 'That bullet . . .'

'Luis Chavez happened,' said Ethan, pulling at Klaus's shoulders. 'He was trying to take Nelson hostage. There was a struggle and the gun went off. Heck. We're getting awful low . . .'

Alec stared ahead in horrified fascination. The dense jungle was rushing up to meet them at a terrifying speed. He undid his seat belt and tried to help Ethan pull Klaus back in his seat; but as he took hold of the pilot's arm, he moaned and lifted his head.

'What happened?' he gasped.

'You've been shot,' said Ethan. 'We've got to get the nose of this plane up fast or we're going to crash.'

Klaus nodded but he didn't seem to take it in. 'Who . . . ? Who shot me?'

'Never mind that now,' Alec urged him. 'Try

to—' He broke off in amazement, staring down. He was looking at a large clearing in the midst of the green vegetation, a great rectangle where grey stone cut straight lines through the undergrowth. He saw houses, streets, a marketplace; and then, even more astounding, rearing up from the midst of the stone, a huge step pyramid. Alec's first thought was that it was an ancient ruin, but the plane was low enough now for him to see crowds of people around the base; at the summit, figures dressed in masks and colourful robes were staring up as the plane thundered over them. Above them towered a huge statue of what looked like a skeleton with a hideous grinning skull.

Alec was speechless for a moment – and when he finally opened his mouth to shout something, the pyramid had already dropped away behind them and the plane was over jungle once more. He turned to look at Ethan but the American was intent on getting Klaus out of the way and it was clear he had seen nothing.

Alec decided that this was no time to dwell on what he might or might not have seen. Right now there were more pressing matters.

'Klaus!' he yelled into the German's ear.

'You've got to pull the plane up. We're going to crash!'

Klaus's ice-blue eyes flickered as he seemed to register Alec's words. He nodded and began to pull back on the joystick. The plane's nose came up a little and the descent slowed. But Alec could see that the pilot was barely conscious. There was a thick sheen of sweat on his face and his teeth were gritted against the pain of the bullet. Alec stole a glance and saw that the back of his shirt was soaked with blood.

'You'll have to take over the controls, Ethan,' he shouted.

Ethan was studying them doubtfully. 'I'm not sure,' he said. 'This isn't like any plane I've ever flown.'

'I'm all right,' gasped Klaus. 'I . . . can do this . . . really. We just need to keep heading south-east and—' His eyes suddenly rolled back and he slumped forward again, his hands still clutching the joystick. The plane went into another dive, almost throwing Alec and Ethan into the windscreen. As he pushed himself upright, Alec registered that the canopy of the trees was perilously close. Flocks of birds were flapping up into the air, alarmed by the roar of the engine.

'We've got to get him out of his seat!' he cried.

Ethan had managed to get Klaus's seat belt undone and was tugging furiously at his shoulders, but he was still slumped over the joystick, his hands gripping it as though trying to protect it. Alec heard a dull thud as the plane's wheels clipped a chunk of foliage from the treetops.

'Ethan!' he gasped. 'Try to—'

'Too late!' Ethan yelled back at him. 'Brace yourself for impact.'

Alec saw what looked like a green ocean rising up to meet them. He threw out his arms and hooked them around the back of the co-pilot's seat, and then the undercarriage ploughed through the treetops. Alec was just telling himself that it wasn't as bad as he'd expected when the propeller slammed into something more substantial and shattered. A large sliver of wood careened off the windshield and went spinning away. Then there was a great grinding roar as the Junkers, carried along by its own momentum, crashed headlong through leaves and twigs and branches.

Suddenly there was a massive impact that shook Alec's body to the core and the plane's left wing was ripped away with a sound like an explosion. Then there was a long, buffeting, shaking tumble, which threatened to throw Alec backwards into the cabin, but he clung onto the seat until he thought his arms would be torn from their sockets. Another impact shuddered through the plane and it began to whirl around in a mad, dizzying circle, thundering down through humid darkness, tearing through the trees before striking what felt like solid ground. Then it began to slide along on its belly, glancing off a series of tree trunks as it went. One side of the fuselage was suddenly opened up like a tin can and Alec dimly registered a scream of terror from somewhere behind him, but then, at last, the plane eased to a halt.

There was a long silence. Alec remembered to let go of the seat and slumped onto the floor. He saw that Ethan was still hanging onto Klaus's seat. The windscreen had shattered and the cockpit was filled with a mad jumble of branches. One stout tree limb had come within inches of Klaus's chest. Alec turned and gazed around the dark, smoke-filled cabin. His nostrils filled with the stench of petrol. He could see that three of the seated passengers were still strapped in, but

Coates and Frank Campbell were lying in an untidy heap at the very back of the plane. As he looked, the two men stirred and began to disentangle themselves from each other.

'Everybody all right?' he asked fearfully, but the only replies he got were a few groans.

'Everybody out, quick as you can!' announced Ethan, from behind him. 'This thing could blow! Alec, give me a hand with Klaus.'

Alec nodded. He tried to stand up but realized that his whole body was shaking with adrenalin. He gritted his teeth, got himself upright and stumbled towards Klaus. Together, he and Ethan manoeuvred him up from his seat and dragged him out through the ragged opening in the plane's side. They fell to the ground, which was wet and boggy underfoot, and carried the German a safe distance away. Alec knew from his own experience that crashed planes had a tendency to explode and he didn't want to be standing next to this one if it did.

As they stumbled off through the undergrowth, Coates came stumbling out through a rip in the side of the fuselage and almost fell to the ground. Alec saw that he had a deep gash across his forehead and blood was coursing down his face. He was quickly followed by the other passengers. Ulysses T. Nelson was still holding a hand to one ear. Frank helped a sobbing Conchita out, one arm curled protectively around her shoulders. Last of all came Luis Chavez, his face pale. He gazed around at the devastation he had caused as though unable to believe his eyes. He looked this way and that, and finally saw Alec and Ethan setting Klaus down on the ground. He hurried towards them.

'How is he?' he gasped.

'Still alive, no thanks to you,' snapped Ethan. 'You hit him in the back.'

'Oh no . . .' Luis was shaking his head. 'It was an accident. Nobody was supposed to get hurt. I only wanted—'

'Save your breath,' Ethan told him. He propped Klaus forward into a sitting position, then took a hunting knife from his belt and slit the back of his shirt open, revealing the entry wound, a round hole the size of a sovereign.

Alec winced. It looked serious. Ethan tore a strip of the shirt away, folded it into a wad and pressed it hard against the wound. He looked up and saw that the others were settling themselves down only a few feet away from the wreckage.

Thick smoke was pouring from the open hatch. 'I'd advise you all to move further away!' he shouted. 'That plane could go up any minute!'

Everybody obeyed him instantly, stumbling and tripping through the dense vegetation. Coates was mopping at his bloody forehead with a clean white handkerchief. In his other hand he carried a pistol – which, Alec assumed, must have belonged to Luis Chavez. He came over and looked at Klaus doubtfully.

The German stirred, moaned and his eyes flickered open. He looked around, and then his gaze fell on the shattered remains of the Junkers.

'Oh no,' he said. He started to get up but a spasm of pain lanced through him and he dropped back against Ethan with a grunt.

Luis moved forward to kneel before him. 'Señor Dorfmann,' he said, 'I am so sorry. You have to believe me, it was a mistake, I never meant for any of this to happen.' He looked pleadingly at Alec. 'You believe me, don' you? I was just trying to kidnap Señor Nelson.'

Alec stared at him. 'But why?' he asked. 'Why would you do something like that?'

'So I could help to save this.' He gestured at the dense forest all around them. 'So he wouldn't carry on cutting it all down. I tried doing it through legal channels but they just ignored me.' He reached out and grabbed Klaus's sleeve, 'I only wanted to divert your plane,' he said. 'For a few days. Nobody was going to be harmed, that was never the plan.' He pointed towards Frank Campbell. 'But then that maniac jumped me and the gun went off.'

Frank looked over his shoulder in disbelief. 'Oh, *I'm* the maniac, am I? That's great. You was the one waving the gun around, matey. What did you expect me to do, sit there smilin'?' Beside him, Conchita burst into fresh tears and Frank put a consoling arm around her. 'There, there, Conchita, don't you worry now. We'll get you out of here – I'm sure help will be on its way in no time at all.'

Ethan glanced at Alec. 'I don't know what gives him that idea,' he murmured. 'Who the hell is going to find us way out here?'

Klaus groaned again, then glared at Luis Chavez. 'Damn you,' he hissed. 'You have ruined me. That plane was my livelihood. It was all I had.' He coughed, and blood sprayed out of his mouth. He lifted his gaze and saw Coates standing a short distance away, still holding the pistol. 'Give me that gun,' he said.

Coates shook his head. 'Suicide is not the answer,' he said.

'Who said anything about suicide?' snapped Klaus. He jabbed a finger at Luis. 'I'm going to shoot *him*.'

'I understand how you feel,' said Ethan, 'but we can't let you do that.' He studied Klaus for a moment. 'Who knows where we are?'

Klaus squinted up at him. 'Huh?'

'Somebody must know what route we were taking.'

'I mentioned it . . . to my mechanic,' said Klaus.

'That's it? Your mechanic? There's nobody else? No official body, no airport or other authority?'

Klaus forced a laugh through gritted teeth. 'It's a one-man show, Mr Wade. I cut a lot of . . . corners. Have to if it's going to work financially. And besides, even if people knew . . . the route we were taking . . . it would be like trying to find the needle in the . . . in the . . .'

'Haystack?' said Alec, trying to be helpful. He looked at the dank green forest. 'So we're lost? Is that what you're saying?'

Klaus nodded. 'Done for,' he muttered. He

glared at Luis again. 'You might as well have put a bullet in each one of us.'

'Look,' said Luis, 'I already told you, I—'

He broke off in alarm as a hand closed on his collar and jerked him to his feet. He turned to be met by a punch in the face from a powerful right hand, and sprawled to the ground. Nelson stood over him, his fists raised.

'You dirty little sneak, I ought to beat you senseless,' he snarled. 'Look what you've done, Chavez. Look what you've brought us all to.'

Luis gazed up defiantly at his old enemy and wiped a trickle of blood from the corner of his mouth. 'You should be thanking me, Señor Nelson,' he said. 'You're always in the market for more jungle and now you've got as much as you can handle.'

Nelson launched a savage kick into the ribs of the Mexican, who curled up into a foetal position with a howl of pain.

'Not so tough now, are ya?' taunted the oil man. 'You greasy little cockroach, I should have paid somebody to take you out years ago. But no, I tried to do it by the book. And look where it's got me!' He lifted his foot to take another kick, but froze at the sound of a pistol being cocked.

He turned in surprise to find that Coates was pointing the gun at him.

'That's enough,' said the Yorkshireman.

Nelson stared at him. 'Are you out of your mind?' he cried. 'You're defending this conniving little sneak? After what he's done, we oughta string him up from the nearest tree.'

Coates shook his head. 'I can assure you, that's not going to happen, Mr Nelson. I understand you're angry, but fighting each other is not going to help us, is it? We need to think about working together. Now move away from him, if you please.'

Nelson shook his head as though he couldn't quite believe what was happening. But after a few moments he went off a little way and sat down on a fallen tree. 'Crazy,' he muttered to nobody in particular. 'Absolutely crazy.'

There was a short silence and then a dull *whump* as something in the wreckage ignited. A gout of oily flame belched out of the fuselage. Conchita jumped to her feet and pointed towards it.

'My costumes!' she shrieked. 'My make-up!'

Frank looked at her in alarm.

'I need them for the screen test!' she howled.

He nodded and started towards the wreckage. 'Don't worry, Conchita, I know exactly where they are,' he said. 'I'll get 'em.'

'Where the hell are you going?' Ethan yelled after him.

'Conchita's stuff,' said Frank. 'She needs it.'

'Don't be stupid! Stay where you are!'

But Frank was still heading for the plane. Ethan took Alec's hand and pressed it down on the bloody rag he'd been holding against Klaus's back. Then he jumped to his feet and ran across the intervening space. He dived at Frank's legs and brought him roughly to the ground.

'Let me up!' said Frank. 'I just need to—'

The rest of his words were lost as the plane's petrol tank ignited and it erupted in a great orange blaze. Alec felt the shock wave rush by him and heard Klaus's last lamenting cry as his most prized possession blew apart in front of him. When he looked down at the German, he saw tears running down his dirty face.

He reached out and squeezed Klaus's arm. 'It was a fabulous plane,' he said quietly. 'I'm really sorry.'

He glanced across at Ethan and Frank. They were sitting up now, both of them staring at the great column of fire and smoke rising through the trees.

Meanwhile Conchita was marching backwards and forwards, her little hands bunched into fists. 'Now what am I gonna do?' she shouted. 'I can't audition for Señor Mayer looking like this!'

Coates sighed and shook his head. He moved across to Alec. 'She's got about as much chance of making her blessed screen test tomorrow as I have of becoming lead dancer with the Bolshoi Ballet,' he murmured. He gazed around hopelessly, as though seeking inspiration; finding none, he slipped the pistol into the waistband of his trousers and crouched down beside Klaus. 'One thing's for sure,' he said. 'We're going to have to try and get the bullet out of this fellow's back. Master Alec, this isn't going to be pleasant,' he said. 'You might want to move away a little.'

But Alec shook his head. 'I'll stay with him,' he said.

Coates nodded. Together he and Alec rolled the German gently onto his side, then he lifted the shirt to reveal the wound. Using his handkerchief, he mopped away the worst of the blood.

'How does it look?' grunted Klaus.

'I've seen worse,' said Coates, but his expression was grim. He glanced at Alec. 'Would you be so kind as to go and ask Mr Wade for his knife?' he murmured.

Alec nodded. Ethan was coming back towards them.

'Coates needs your knife,' said Alec. 'He's going to try and dig the bullet out.'

Ethan frowned, but he drew the big Bowie knife he always carried at his belt. 'We'll need to make a fire so we can heat the blade up first,' he said. He glanced around. 'At least there's no shortage of wood here. We'll just need to poke a branch into the wreckage of the plane to get a light.' He shook his head. 'This is a fine fix we're in . . .'

'We'll be all right, won't we?' said Alec. 'I mean, somebody will come looking for the plane eventually, won't they?'

Ethan didn't say anything for a moment. 'Let's get that fire started,' he suggested finally. 'Then we'll see what's to be done.'

CHAPTER EIGHT

A Pow-wow

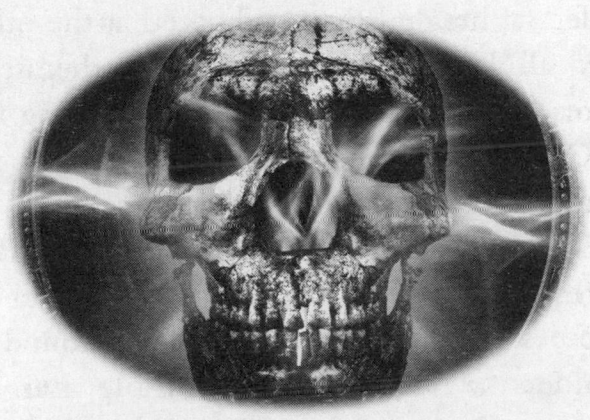

Ethan found a clearing dotted with fallen tree trunks and called everybody over to discuss the situation. As they sat down, they were all horribly aware of Klaus, stretched out in the shade of the trees a short distance from the fire. He had passed out some time ago and had not awoken since.

The crude operation that had finally removed the bullet from his back had been terrible to behold. Coates had been obliged to dig deep with the point of the red-hot blade, but despite the pain, Klaus had gritted his teeth and refused to cry out. Eventually the bullet had emerged, but not before the pilot had lost a massive amount of blood. It had been a mercy when he finally lost consciousness.

Alec sat beside Ethan and gazed at the others. They all looked pretty sorry for themselves. Coates had managed to stem the bleeding from his forehead, but the side of his face was a mass of dark bruises. Conchita couldn't seem to stop crying; her glamorous blouse and skirt looked not only dirty but faintly ridiculous in this remote setting. Frank had his arm around her shoulders as he tried to console her. His expensive Panama suit was ripped and stained, and the patch of blood at his shoulder indicated that he too had been injured in the crash. Ulysses T. Nelson sat with his arms crossed, glaring angrily around at the others as though he blamed them for what had happened and resented being in their company. Luis Chavez sat slightly apart, his face pale, shoulders slumped, looking as if he wished it was him and not Klaus who had taken a bullet in the back. Despite what had happened, Alec felt a certain degree of pity for him. He felt sure that the Mexican had not intended any of this to happen.

Ethan looked slowly around at the group, his

expression grim. 'I guess I don't have to tell you that this is serious,' he said. 'We've come down in one of the most remote spots in Mexico. From what Klaus told me before he passed out, there's hardly anyone knows where we are and the chances of somebody else flying over this spot are low.' He gestured up at the thick canopy above their heads. 'And even if they did, the likelihood of being spotted from the air is zilch.'

There was a long silence while this information sank in.

Frank pointed towards the still blazing wreckage of the plane and the thick column of smoke rising through the trees. 'Surely somebody's going to see that!' he reasoned.

'It's possible,' admitted Ethan. 'But even if a plane *did* come by this way, there's nowhere for it to land.'

'Well, what do you suggest?' snarled Nelson irritably. 'We just sit here and wait to die?'

'I'm not saying that. No, the way I see it, the only chance we have is to walk.'

'Walk?' Frank looked amused by this statement. 'Walk where? You saw how big this bloomin' rainforest is. How would we even know which direction to take?'

Ethan shrugged. 'We'd come to a river eventually. Rivers flow out to the sea, so we'd just have to follow that and hope we could get to the coast.'

'Great idea,' said Nelson dismissively. 'Who put you in charge of this operation, cowboy?'

'I'm not in charge,' said Ethan. 'I'm just the man with a plan. You've got a better one, then speak up.'

Nelson scowled. 'Well, if we had a way of knowing where we are,' he said, 'we'd have a better chance than just wandering.'

Alec remembered something and reached into his pocket. 'I've got this,' he said. He pulled out a small compass that his father had given him for his last birthday. He lifted the brass cover to reveal the glass face beneath.

The oil man snorted derisively. 'Oh, now we'll be fine. We've got a kid's toy. Yippie doodle day!'

'It's not a *toy*,' Alec assured him. 'It's a real compass.'

'Great,' said Nelson. 'You'll excuse me if I don't dance for joy. This isn't a boy scouts' convention, sonny, this is serious stuff.'

'At least Master Alec thought to bring a compass,' said Coates. 'What have you got to offer?'

Nelson didn't answer so Coates turned his attention to Ethan. 'What are we going to do about Herr Dorfmann?' he asked.

Ethan looked puzzled. 'Do about him?' he muttered. 'What do you mean?'

'Well, if we're going to try and walk out of here, he's hardly in any condition to join us, is he? We'll have to make some kind of stretcher.'

Ethan frowned. 'That's a tall order,' he said. 'We don't have any tools. And besides . . .'

'Yes?' said Coates.

Ethan lowered his voice, just in case Klaus was awake now. 'That bullet hit a lung — that's why he's coughing up blood. I doubt he'll last the night.'

Alec stared at him. 'But . . . Coates got the bullet out. There must be *some* hope.'

'There's always hope,' admitted Ethan.

'Might be better if he does die,' said Nelson brutally. 'If we have to carry him, we'll have no chance.'

'But we *will* carry him,' said Coates, quietly but firmly.

'And if he dies?'

'I will bury him,' announced Luis, speaking for the first time. 'I will do it if I have to dig the grave with my bare hands.'

'Very noble,' said Nelson. 'It's a pity you didn't think about that before you started waving a gun around. Thanks to you, there could be a few more graves to dig before much longer!'

Conchita stared at him for a moment, then threw back her head in despair. 'We are going to die here!' she cried.

'Did you have to say that?' complained Frank.

'I'm just telling it like it is,' said Nelson. 'Could you get that damned woman to quieten down? Her blubbing is getting on my nerves.'

If Nelson had punched Conchita in the face, Frank couldn't have looked more horrified. 'How *dare* you?' he said. 'Can't you see she's upset?'

'We're all upset,' snapped Nelson. 'But we're not making a song and dance about it.'

'I'll thank you to keep a civil tongue in your head,' said Frank. 'Let's not forget that we are gentlemen and this is the only lady in our party. The last thing she needs to hear is that kind of talk.'

'Oh, excuse me,' said Nelson. 'I was forgetting what a classy dame she is.'

Conchita stopped crying and fixed him with a look that could have stripped varnish from a grand piano. 'You shut up your mouth, big shot!' she shrieked. 'You not so fancy I can't give you a big kick in the pants!'

'Yeah, like you were saying, a real lady!' mocked Nelson; and Frank started to get up, fists bunched.

Ethan raised his hands to try and calm everyone down but it was Alec who jumped to his feet.

'This is ridiculous!' he shouted, and everybody turned to look at him. 'Don't you know how serious this is? The last thing we need is everybody falling out and arguing. We won't last five minutes like that.' He glared around at them. 'We've got to work together if we're to have any chance. If we can't do that we may as well just lie down and wait to die.'

There was a long silence after he had spoken. Nelson looked as though he was about to say something, but then he bowed his head and looked at his feet. Alec sat down again and Ethan patted him on the shoulder.

'Funny how it takes a fifteen-year-old kid to tell it like it is,' he said.

'Sixteen,' said Alec quietly, and Ethan nodded. He looked around at the others.

'Now,' he said. 'Before the plane came down, Klaus said we were flying south-east . . .' He pointed at Alec's compass. 'There's no telling how far it is to the coast. But if we walk north-west, we will at least be heading back the way we came; and I seem to recall flying over quite a few rivers on the way here.'

'What do we do when we reach a river?' asked Coates politely. 'Swim?'

'No, we'd have to build a raft or a boat, I guess.'

'And you'd know how to do that?'

'I never have, but we'd just have to figure it out. It's the only thing I can think of. If anybody has any other suggestions, speak up.'

'I think maybe I have a better plan,' said Luis.

'Keep out of this,' growled Nelson. 'Nobody gives a damn what you think, Chavez.'

'Let him speak,' snapped Coates. 'Go on, Mr Chavez.'

Luis looked around nervously before speaking. 'I realize you all blame me for this,' he said. 'And I accept full responsibility. But . . . I have spent many years in the Huasteca Veracruzana. I know how to survive here.' He looked at Ethan. 'I can show you how to find drinking water, I know how to set traps to get the food we need, I speak the language of some of the Indian tribes. If you will let me, *señor*, I will try to make amends for what I have done. And if we make it out of here alive, I will accept any punishment that is coming to me.'

Ethan nodded. 'Seems fair enough,' he said.

'You remember, on the plane I wanted the pilot to change course? I have friends waiting for me at a landing strip in the jungle due west of here, maybe thirty, forty miles. They have equipment, a wireless, a plane . . . I think we would have a better chance of making it there than heading down some unknown river.'

Ethan nodded. 'Sounds like good sense,' he admitted. 'Think you could find your way there?'

'Just a moment,' said Nelson, looking out-raged. 'You're not buying this, are you? He just wants to get me to his people so he can go on with his crackpot kidnap scheme. And who's to say that he'd let any of you people leave? You know too much. You could identify him.'

Luis shook his head. 'I swear to you, Señor Wade, on my mother's grave, I would not betray you. Everything is changed now – a man has been shot and that was never part of the plan. Me and my friends, we only care about the rainforest, about protecting it.'

'Oh yeah, bring out the violins!' said Nelson. 'Give me a break, will ya?'

Ethan sighed. 'Well,' he said, 'I have to say it sounds like a better idea. It's forty miles as against maybe hundreds. What does everybody else think?'

There was a silence while they all considered the question.

'As you say,' muttered Coates at last, 'it does sound more feasible.'

'There's something else to consider,' said Alec, and everyone turned to look at him. 'Something I saw from the plane when we were coming down. I know it sounds ridiculous, but . . . well, there's a city not far from here.'

'A *city*?' echoed Ethan. 'What are you talking about, Alec? There couldn't be, not way out here.'

'I saw it from the plane. You didn't notice because you were trying to get Klaus up out of his seat. It . . . it can't be all that far from here.'

'Don't you mean a *village*?' asked Luis incredulously. 'An Indian village?'

'No, this was built of stone. It looked . . .

ancient. There were houses and streets — and a huge step pyramid right in the middle of it. I saw it.'

Nelson waved a hand in dismissal. 'An ancient ruin,' he said. 'I've heard stories about such places in the jungle. Aztec, most likely, deserted for centuries—'

'No,' said Alec, wanting to be sure there was no mistake about this. 'There were people, lots of them. I think . . . they were watching us as we passed over.'

There was a deep silence for a moment and then Nelson laughed. 'I think somebody's had a little too much sun,' he said.

'No, I swear! I didn't imagine this.' Alec looked at Ethan. 'You didn't see it, but it was there all right. A huge place. Well, they'd have food and water, wouldn't they? They might even give us guides to help us find our way out of here.'

Ethan and Coates exchanged looks.

'What do you think?' Ethan asked him.

'If Master Alec says he saw a city, then I believe him,' Coates said. 'But it may not be as straight-forward as he thinks.'

'How do you mean?'

Coates frowned. 'Well, he's assuming that the

119

people in this place are friendly – but there's no reason to suppose they are. They could be hostile. Some of the tribes out here . . . well, you hear stories about them, don't you? They practise cannibalism and all sorts.'

'Cannibalism?' said Conchita, mystified. She looked at Frank. 'What is this?'

Frank looked away. 'Oh, nothin' to worry about, my dear, it's just . . .'

'It's just people eating each other,' said Nelson flatly, then smiled triumphantly at the look of terror on her face.

'Eating people? Oh no, this cannot be!'

'Well, let's not go jumping to conclusions,' Coates said. 'I'm only saying, you hear stories.' He looked at Luis. 'You'd probably know more about that kind of thing . . .'

Luis shrugged. 'Some of the fierce tribes will eat their enemies,' he said. 'Not the whole body, you understand, just their hearts and maybe their livers.'

'Can we please change the subject?' snapped Frank. 'Conchita does not want to hear that sort of thing, thank you very much!'

Ethan nodded. 'She's not the only one,' he said. 'Well, maybe we'd be better trying for Luis's airstrip. At least he knows the people there are friendly.'

'Friendly!' exclaimed Nelson. 'These are the ones who were planning on cutting my head off!'

'We weren't really going to do that,' protested Luis. 'We would only *threaten* to. You'd have been released unharmed once our demands were met.'

'Yeah, sure,' muttered Nelson.

Ethan frowned. 'Well, Luis figures forty miles to the airstrip. That's one heck of a way to walk, especially if we're carrying a wounded man. There's part of me that says we should at least check out what Alec saw. Kid, how far away you figure this city is?'

Alec spread his hands in a gesture of helplessness. He tried to cast his mind back to the time that might have elapsed between seeing the city and the plane crashing into the treetops, but everything was a blur. 'Hard to say. It seemed like we flew over it only . . . ten minutes before we went down, but . . . I don't know, it could have been longer. I don't think it would be more than a day's walk.'

Ethan nodded and looked around thoughtfully. 'Well, we ain't going anywhere today,' he decided. 'It's already getting late and we need to see what we can salvage from the plane. There won't be much of anything left inside, but I'd say we lost quite a bit of stuff as we came down.' He pointed to the vegetation behind the plane. 'The fuselage was ripped open when we hit the trees – I figure some things must have fallen out. I want everybody to help out on this. Look for anything we might be able to use – luggage, tools, food, rope, whatever. We'll camp here tonight and head out at first light.'

Luis stood up. 'I respectfully ask that I might be excused,' he said.

Nelson directed a withering look at him. 'What's the matter, Mr Naturalist?' he said. 'Too frail for a little hard work?'

Luis shook his head. 'Not at all,' he said. 'But if we're going to start walking tomorrow, we will need to have something to eat tonight. I'll take care of that.' He stood up and headed off into the jungle. Everybody watched till he was out of sight. Then Nelson turned to glare at Ethan.

'Please tell me you're not letting that little cockroach fool you,' he said. 'He's already proved he's not to be trusted.'

Ethan gazed back at him. 'I won't pretend he's

my favourite person,' he said. 'He's responsible for all this, and if we make it back to civilization, he'll have to answer for it. But on the other hand, he's the closest we've got to an expert on this kind of country and we'd be mighty foolish to string him up like you wanted.' He looked around. 'Come on, everyone. We need to get searching before nightfall.'

Everyone got up except Conchita, who sat there on her tree trunk, snivelling quietly to herself.

'Miss Velez . . . ?' prompted Ethan, and she looked up at him indignantly.

'What?' she snapped. 'You . . . you don' expect me to help, do you?'

'I don't see why not,' he told her.

'But I . . . I am Conchita Velez. Frank, tell him who I am!'

'I know who you are,' Ethan assured her. 'But things have changed now. We all have to help. The first thing you need to do is find some suitable clothes for yourself.'

'Clothes?' She looked at him as though she couldn't believe her ears. 'I *have* clothes! Very nice clothes.'

'Yes, and I'm sure they look great around the

nightspots of Acapulco,' he told her. 'But pretty soon it's going to be dusk, and when that happens, there's going to be a million insects swarming though these bushes. If they find you with those bare arms and legs, you are gonna be the best free dinner they ever had.'

Conchita blanched. She got up and allowed Frank to take her arm, picking her way through the undergrowth with exaggerated care. The two of them made for the long swathe of damaged vegetation where the plane had cut through the jungle. Nelson followed them.

Ethan shook his head and looked at Alec and Coates. 'This promises to be a lot of fun,' he said bleakly.

Alec frowned. 'I'm really sorry,' he said. 'If I hadn't persuaded Coates to come out looking for that Olmec head, none of this would have happened.' He thought for a moment. 'Well, I suppose the plane crash might still have happened, but we wouldn't have been on board.'

Ethan shrugged his shoulders. 'Well, no use crying over spilled milk,' he said. 'We're here now and the only thing we can do is try our very best to get out of it in one piece.'

Coates sighed. 'They'll be getting worried that

we haven't returned,' he said bleakly. 'They'll doubtless be thinking about contacting Master Alec's father. I shouldn't be at all surprised if I get the sack over this.'

Ethan slapped a hand on Coates's shoulder. 'Right now,' he said, 'I'd say that's the least of your worries. Come on, let's get looking.'

He and Coates started off after the others. Alec stood there for a moment, gazing after them. He was experiencing a strange mixture of feelings. Most of him felt really sorry for what had happened. But a small part of him couldn't stop thinking about the mysterious city the plane had passed over; and hoping that before very much longer he'd get a better look at it.

CHAPTER NINE
The Dawning

A lec opened his eyes and was surprised by the dull wash of daylight. It felt as though he had been asleep only moments. He was looking at the smouldering remains of the campfire, over which the frazzled carcass of a young tapir still hung, already covered in a thick mantle of buzzing insects. Luis had provided the meat, which he had caught in some kind of snare; they'd all eaten ravenously, even Nelson — though he could not quite bring himself to thank Luis for providing the food. They had passed an uncomfortable night, listening to the sounds of the jungle: the shrieking of monkeys, the roaring of jaguars, and myriad unseen insects that chirruped and whined and buzzed all around them.

Conchita had at least managed to find some more suitable clothing from the luggage strewn in the plane's wake – a pair of men's trousers, an oversized khaki shirt and even a battered slouch hat. She looked odd to say the least, but woe betide anyone who commented on it.

After they had eaten their fill, the group had started bickering again and Alec had eventually drifted off with the sounds of an argument ringing in his ears.

He lifted his head and looked around. A pale mist hung low over the small clearing where they had camped and the faint dawn light was only just beginning to filter through the canopy of trees overhead. He saw the others, slumped in awkward positions around the pile of grey ash, and thought about snuggling down and catching another hour of sleep, but something stopped him. He reached out a hand and scratched at his arm, where some insects had left a couple of nasty bites.

Something was wrong, and for the moment he wasn't sure what it was. He sat up and peered this way and that, but nothing seemed out of place. Then it occurred to him. The silence. In nearly every country he'd ever visited, the dawn was greeted by the sounds of birds calling; but here there was nothing – not even the creatures he had heard in the night. He glanced at Ethan, lying only a short distance away from him, and thought of shaking him awake, but decided he might want to sleep on. Maybe the dawns were always silent in the Huasteca Veracruzana.

He got quietly to his feet and moved across to where Klaus was lying. To his dismay he saw that somebody had pulled the sheet of canvas they had been using as a blanket up over the pilot's face. Alec remembered that Coates had been sitting with him late last night. Clearly the German's suffering was now over. Alec pulled back the canvas a little and saw that he was gazing sightlessly up at the forest canopy above his head. When Alec placed a finger against his throat, there was no sign of any pulse. He sighed and gently covered the pilot's face again; he felt a terrible sadness overcome him. He had only known Klaus for a short while, but he had seemed a decent enough fellow; and he had saved Alec's life.

It must have happened in the night, while Alec was sleeping. He walked to the edge of the clearing and gazed thoughtfully into the dense undergrowth, but he couldn't see very far in any direction. He wondered how many miles they would have to walk before they discovered the city he had glimpsed from the plane. He asked himself if they would ever get out of here alive. He couldn't help feeling responsible for the situation. Why, oh why was he so strong-willed? Why had he insisted on dragging Coates out into the middle of nowhere to look at that blasted stone head?

He felt a sudden need to relieve himself, and not wanting to disturb anyone, tiptoed as quietly as possible into the jungle. When he had gone a short distance, he ducked behind a group of tall ferns and unbuttoned his trousers. He was just buttoning himself back up when he heard something moving slowly through the bushes away to his left. He froze, then turned his head to stare through the screen of ferns. What he saw made his heart pound in his chest.

An Indian was creeping furtively towards the clearing, gliding through the undergrowth like a ghost. The man was tall and wiry, his long jet-black hair cut in a fringe across his forehead. Alec saw that he had bright red stone plugs through his earlobes and another through his nostrils. He was naked except for a loincloth and a few items of jewellery, and carried a long wooden spear tipped with a deadly stone head.

Alec fought down a rising wave of panic. There was another sound to his right and he saw a second warrior, almost an exact copy of the first. He too was creeping forward, armed with a wooden club glinting with chunks of black obsidian.

Alec stood there in a fog of uncertainty. His first instinct was to run, but he knew he couldn't just desert his friends. His eyes flicked back towards the clearing, and through the screen of ferns he saw that everyone was still sleeping, quite unaware of the danger creeping up on them.

His first thought was to run out yelling his head off in the hope that he might wake the others up in time – but he immediately realized that it was already too late for that. So he ducked down and stayed exactly where he was, telling himself that if he was going to be of help to his friends, he needed to stay concealed. He watched in mute horror as more Indians crept up on the sleeping survivors. There were eight of them in all.

It was over in moments. Coates woke up and was immediately overpowered. He struggled but was thrown down onto his face and his hands were tied behind his back. As Alec watched helplessly, the same fate was meted out to the others. Ethan had been sleeping slightly apart from the rest; he began to resist, and one of the Indians raised a club to strike him. Alec began to move forward – but then an authoritative voice shouted something in a language he didn't understand and the Indian lowered the club. Alec dropped back down behind the bushes. As he watched, Ethan too was flipped over onto his front and his hands secured. One of the Indians took his Bowie knife away and then grabbed his pistol from its holster. He seemed to know that it was a weapon.

Ethan twisted his head to one side and tried talking to his captors. 'Hey, it's OK, we're friendly. We come in peace! There's no need for this! Luis, talk to them, for Pete's sake!'

Luis tried a few lines of a native tongue; when

that seemed to get no reaction, he tried another.

The warriors didn't respond at all. Their faces were impassive, but for the moment at least, it didn't seem as if they meant their captives any harm.

'There's absolutely no reason to do this,' said Coates, one cheek flat against the earth. 'We . . . are . . . friends. Friends, understand?'

The Indian securing Coates's hands shouted something that didn't sound very complimentary and slapped the back of his head with one hand. Then he grabbed his arm and jerked him upright. He was pushed towards the others, who were all being roped together, as if they were setting out on a mountaineering expedition. Ethan was looking around, an expression of impotent fury on his face. He had lost his Stetson in the scuffle and looked odd without it.

'Where's Alec?' he whispered to Coates; the valet could only shrug his big shoulders. The two of them began to scan the surrounding under-growth, trying not to make it too obvious what they were doing.

The Indians finished roping their captives together. Conchita was crying and struggling, and they seemed fascinated by her: they were pulling at her hair and laughing at her horrified reaction, but they soon stopped when she slammed her shoulder into one of them and yelled at him.

'Take your hands off me, you pig!' she screamed.

The Indians retreated a little, looking wary, clearly not used to such feisty females. Then Alec saw that one of them was crouched beside Klaus's body. He was prodding the German with the butt of his spear, puzzled by his lack of response. He looked up at his companions and made a gesture, jerking the thumb of one hand across his throat.

Ethan gazed down at the body in evident surprise.

'He slipped away in the night,' Coates told him. 'I didn't see any point in waking you up.'

Ethan grunted. 'Too bad,' he said. 'He seemed like a swell guy.' He was still looking furtively around. At one point he was staring straight towards Alec's hiding place and Alec considered giving some kind of signal, but then thought better of it. He couldn't risk giving himself away. The Indian left Klaus's body where it was and went back to join his companions.

'Surely they're not just going to leave him here?' said Ethan. 'Luis, try talking to them again. Ask if they'll let us bury him.'

The Mexican nodded and fired off a few questions, but the Indians just looked at him uncomprehendingly. He tried another dialect and then another, but still got no reaction. Eventually one of them said something to him in a strange sing-song tongue, but Luis seemed equally baffled.

'They're not speaking a Huasteca dialect,' he said. 'It sounds like Nahuatl, but it is very different to any I've heard before.'

'Oh, wonderful,' said Coates. 'So good to have an expert with us. What's Na-wattle, exactly?'

Alec, in hiding, knew the answer to that one before Luis supplied it.

'It's the language of the Aztecs,' the Mexican said.

'Oh good, so we've been captured by Aztecs,' said Coates. 'Marvellous. What are we supposed to do now?'

Alec knew that these people couldn't be actual Aztecs. As far as he was aware, they had died out hundreds of years earlier. But he also knew that many modern-day Indians spoke a version of the language, one that had become mixed with the Spanish spoken by the people who had conquered them.

'Well, they don't seem to mean us any real harm,' said Ethan. 'If they'd wanted to kill us, they could have done so easily. So I guess there's no need for anyone to get too excited.'

'Yeah, but they aren't exactly welcoming us with open arms either,' muttered Nelson. 'Who knows what horrors they've got lined up for us . . .' He directed a baleful glare at Luis. 'This is all your fault,' he said. 'I'm holding you directly responsible for everything that happens to us.'

Luis could only shrug his shoulders. 'You will forgive me if I don't worry too much about that right now,' he said.

One of the Indians stepped forward and cast an eye over the captives. He was dressed much like the others, but something about his bearing suggested to Alec that he might perhaps be the leader of the group. He inspected Ethan's bonds and seemed satisfied. A second Indian, a man with a long turquoise stone pushed lengthways through his nostrils, came over and dropped a loop around Ethan's neck so that he could be pulled along like a pet dog. He was wearing

Ethan's hat, Alec noticed. Though he had it on back to front, he seemed extremely pleased with it. The leader, meanwhile, went along the row of captives, checking all the knots; as he approached Conchita, she shouted at him.

'Keep away from me,' she warned him. 'You lay one hand on me and you'll be sorry!'

He stared at her for a moment, his eyes narrowed in disapproval. Then he spoke. 'Shut up,' he said; she looked at him in shocked surprise.

Alec couldn't believe his ears. Ethan and Coates exchanged amazed glances.

'You . . . you speak English?' Ethan asked the Indian.

He only smiled mysteriously. Then he turned away and said something to the others. The Indian who held the rope gave it a fierce tug, obliging Ethan and the others to stumble after him. They began to walk into the jungle, passing right by Alec's hiding place. He hugged the ground, hardly daring to breathe; then a jolt of shock went through him as he felt something brushing against his hand. He froze and stared down in terror.

A huge yellow centipede was crawling across

the back of his hand. It was some twelve inches long and had jaws that could have administered a very nasty – and quite probably poisonous – bite. Alec's natural impulse was to shake his arm and fling the thing away but he knew that the keen-eared Indians would hear him; so he just had to stay stock-still, holding his breath while the sweat poured down his face. He watched in disgust as the creature moved slowly up onto his shirt-sleeve. It occurred to him that the thing was heading for his face.

Then Alec heard Coates's voice speaking from just a few feet away. 'Wait!' he said. 'Our friend, the pilot. We can't just leave him there!'

But the Indians took no notice of him. They continued to drag the line of captives behind them until they were out of sight. Alec was dimly aware that the centipede had moved up to his shoulder and was twitching its loathsome feelers towards his face. He could be still no longer. He brushed the thing aside with an exclamation of disgust. It skittered away into the undergrowth.

Alec finally remembered to breathe. He got cautiously to his feet and peered through the undergrowth. He could just see the two Indians who were at the rear of the group, padding along a narrow trail. He lifted a hand to wipe the sweat from his face and then, moving as quietly as he could, began to follow them.

CHAPTER TEN

Captives

The Indians walked through the jungle at a brisk pace. Having heard their leader speak those two words of English, their captives were filled with hope.

'Hey, if you guys can speak our language, tell that trained monkey of yours to give me my hat back!' shouted Ethan.

The remark got no response.

'Can't you tell us where you're taking us?' asked Coates.

The leader, who was walking beside Ethan, lifted a finger to his lips, a clear indication that he wasn't prepared to answer any questions. They had no option but to trudge after the Indians along the narrow trail.

They walked in silence for some time before Ethan spoke again.

'This is screwy,' he muttered. He glanced back at Coates, who was just behind him. 'What do you make of it?' he asked quietly.

'Damned if I know. Luis, what do you think?'

'I can't believe it,' came the reply from further up the line. 'A place this remote – you wouldn't think they'd speak a word of English. And the language they *are* speaking . . .'

'Na-wattle?' prompted Coates.

'Nahuatl, yes. The way they speak it seems . . . pure, somehow. Like they've never encountered any Spanish people.'

'But that doesn't make sense,' said Ethan. 'If they're such a remote tribe, how would they know any English?'

'I don't get it,' Luis told him. 'It's almost as if— *Ow!*'

Ethan turned to look down the line and saw that one of the Indians had just whipped Luis across his back with a thin cane.

Luis said something in Spanish, but the Indian didn't seem to understand.

'Maybe we'd better not talk any more,' said Coates. 'It seems to annoy them.'

Ethan ignored the advice. 'Another screwy thing,' he said. 'They took my gun from me. They seemed to know what that was all right – though I don't know how.'

'Yes, it's very odd,' muttered Coates. He lowered his voice a little. 'I'm more concerned with what might have happened to Master Alec. Where do you suppose he is?'

'My guess is he's hiding out somewhere. And if I know him, he's waiting his chance. That's the kind of kid he is.'

'I hope you're right,' said Coates. 'If those savages have hurt him, I'll—' He broke off, realizing that there was absolutely nothing he could do about the situation. His hands were tied securely behind his back and no amount of struggling would ever undo them.

'He's a tough kid,' Ethan assured him. 'He'll be all right.'

He turned to look at the man who seemed to be the leader. He waited until the man glanced at him and then offered a friendly grin. 'Ethan,' he said. 'My name is Ethan.'

The warrior regarded him impassively. He

either didn't understand or didn't care what Ethan's name was.

Ethan repeated his name a few times. He would have liked to be able to pat his chest or the top of his head as he did so, but he couldn't. 'Me . . . Ethan,' he said once more. 'Ethan.'

'E-tan,' said the Indian, and Ethan grinned.

'Yeah, that's right, you got it. E-tan!' Then he nodded his head at the man. '*Your* name?' he asked. No reaction. 'Your . . . name?'

The man shrugged. 'Tlaloc,' he said.

'Tlaloc,' echoed Ethan. 'Tlaloc, good!'

'That's an Aztec name,' announced Luis's voice from back up the line. 'It means . . . of the earth.'

Ethan nodded. 'You . . . leader?' he asked. 'Tlaloc leader?'

Tlaloc, if that was his name, seemed to be tired of all the questions. He lifted a finger to his lips again.

But Ethan pressed on stubbornly. 'How do you speak my language?' he asked. 'How . . . you speak . . . English?'

'Mr Wade, I don't think you should keep pestering the man,' said Coates. 'He's looking decidedly tetchy.'

Ethan ignored the advice. 'Where you take us?' he asked. 'We go to city?'

Tlaloc suddenly seemed to lose patience. He swiped Ethan across the side of the head, nearly knocking him off his feet. 'Shut up!' he said again, and Ethan wondered if these were the only two words of English that he actually knew.

'Hey, cut that out!' he snapped. 'I was only trying to talk to you!'

Tlaloc ignored the remark.

'Better quieten down,' Coates advised him. 'That fellow doesn't beat about the bush.'

'You can say that again,' said Ethan ruefully. 'Though he seems perfectly happy to beat me about the head.' He wished he could lift a hand to rub his stinging right ear, but it was impossible. He concentrated on walking and didn't try speaking to Tlaloc again. He tried to look back down the line, but the trail was narrow and he couldn't see past the heads of the others.

He was hoping against hope that Alec was out there somewhere; and that he knew what he was doing.

Alec kept following the line of Indians and their captives, being careful to stay just the right distance behind them, ready to dive for cover if one of them should look back down the trail.

As he walked, he tried to think what he might do to secure his friends' release. It had occurred to him that if darkness fell and they settled down to sleep, he might be able to creep up and cut their bonds, but he doubted whether he could do it quietly enough to avoid waking up the Indians – and anyway, wouldn't they post guards to keep watch?

Then he realized that if the Indians were heading for the city he had seen from the plane, they might well be there before nightfall – and how could he ever hope to move through a place like that without being seen?

Alec hesitated as he noticed something beside the trail up ahead of him – a grey stone statue some four feet tall rearing up out of the vegetation. As he approached it, he realized that it was Aztec in origin. It was what was called a *chacmool*, and depicted the kneeling figure of a warrior holding a round stone dish. Alec knew from his studies that this was something the Aztecs would have used to make offerings to their gods; he told himself that it must have been hundreds of years old, though the stone looked like it had been carved only recently. He would have hurried straight on by had he not noticed a great swarm of flies buzzing around the stone dish. He approached it slowly and saw to his horror that it was half filled with a thick pool of coagulating blood.

Then he looked down at the feet of the statue and saw a pile of bones, some old and weathered, some relatively new. It was evident that somebody had been making sacrifices here in the last day or so.

But how could such a thing be possible? The worship of Aztec gods was something that belonged in a history book; yet here was evidence that, in this dense rainforest at least, time had stood still. Despite the awful heat, Alec could feel a chill running down his spine.

He glanced up again and realized that he could no longer see the column of people he had been following. They had vanished into the jungle as if by magic – there was no sign of them ever having passed that way. He broke into a run, peering ahead, ready to stop if he came upon them again. After a few minutes he reached a place where several trails led off in different directions. He looked this way and that, hoping to spot some movement, but he saw nothing more than some brightly coloured butterflies, flapping silently in a shaft of sunlight . . . He'd lost them.

Panic took him for a moment: he was lost in a vast, featureless jungle and had no idea which direction to take. Then he remembered his compass and pulled it out, trying to recall which direction the plane had been flying in. He thought Klaus had said something about heading south-east . . . So, he told himself, if he walked north-west, he should be heading towards the city, shouldn't he?

He flipped the compass around until he found a north-west heading and selected the trail that was closest to that. He started walking again, telling himself not to panic, but after what felt like hours of trudging along the narrow path, there was still no sight or sound of the others. He came to a small clearing with a tall tree and looked thoughtfully up into its branches. There were plenty of limbs within easy reach – way up in the tree, he thought, he should to be able to see for miles in all directions.

He slipped the compass into his pocket, and then, reaching up for the first handholds, started to climb . . .

★ ★ ★

They had been walking for hours. To Ethan it seemed as if they were just wandering aimlessly, but the Indians kept up a steady pace and seemed to know exactly where they were going. Around midday, when the sun was at its hottest, Tlaloc called a halt and they were allowed to sit down in a circle for a while. They were all sweating profusely and were grateful when a couple of the Indians went round with a water skin, allowing each of them a mouthful of its tepid contents.

'Quite delicious, thank you,' said Coates as the water was taken away. 'And may I congratulate you on your wonderful presentation?'

'I wouldn't be so sarcastic if I were you,' Nelson warned him. 'For all we know, they understand every word we say.'

'I wouldn't bet on it,' said Coates. 'I think they have a few simple phrases, no more.'

'Yes, but where could they have learned them?' Ethan asked him.

'I really couldn't say, Mr Wade. Perhaps they pop into the nightclubs in Veracruz every weekend for a Charleston session.'

Ethan laughed. 'You kill me, Coates,' he said.

'Even in a tight spot like this, you just don't stop, do you?'

'I try to lift the spirits,' said Coates flatly.

The Indian wearing Ethan's Stetson went over to Conchita and signalled that she should open her mouth and tilt back her head. She did as she was told and received her meagre ration, but wasn't content to leave it at that. 'I need more,' she told him. 'More, *comprende*? Frank, tell him it is not enough!'

Frank looked up at Stetson. 'She needs more water,' he said. 'Savvy? Give the lady more water!' He nodded his head frantically at Conchita. '*Encore!*' he shouted. '*Encore de l'eau!*'

The Indian nodded as though he understood and Conchita tilted back her head in readiness; whereupon the Indian splashed water all over her face, making her gasp for breath. Stetson walked away, laughing delightedly at his childish joke while Conchita stared after him, outraged.

'How dare you!' she shrieked. 'That is no way to treat a lady, you pig! Frank, are you gonna let him get away with that?'

'Frank's in no position to do much about it,' Ethan pointed out. 'Just calm down and figure you got the best of the deal. I wouldn't have minded a little water in the kisser myself.'

Conchita glared at him. 'I don' believe this!' she complained. 'I should be in Tonala now. I should be sipping a Margarita outside my hotel; instead I am here with a bunch of losers, kidnapped by savages.'

Coates favoured her with a tight-lipped smile. 'Much as I agree with the main thrust of your argument,' he said, 'I can't help feeling that referring to us as "losers" is a tad unkind.'

'If you people had not come, this would never have happened,' insisted Conchita.

'How do you arrive at that conclusion?' Ethan asked her. 'Luis would still have been on the plane, he'd still have pulled a gun on Nelson, and chances are you'd still have crashed, only you wouldn't have us around to take care of you.'

'Oh yeah, you takin' *real* good care of me,' growled Conchita. 'Idiot.'

'Ignore her,' said Nelson. 'Let's see what we can salvage out of this situation. Does anybody have any idea which direction we're heading?'

'We are travelling north–west,' said Luis. 'I can tell that much from the position of the sun.'

'Oh, of course, I was forgetting we have the

great expert naturalist with us. Oh well, that's a weight off my mind.'

'Can't you two give it a rest for a moment?' pleaded Ethan. 'I don't want the last thing I ever hear to be the sound of you two bickering.'

'What you mean by that?' asked Conchita fearfully. 'Frank, what does he mean? Why would it be the last thing we ever hear?'

Ethan sighed. 'Lady, I don't want to be Mr Wet Blanket here, but this isn't looking very promising. You must have seen that thing back up the trail. The blood and bones around that altar?'

'Yes – so somebody killed a chicken there or something,' said Conchita. 'That don' mean nothing.'

Ethan looked at her. 'Lady, they weren't chicken bones,' he said. 'We've been kidnapped by what seems to be a bunch of Aztecs and we all know what they're famous for. Believe me, it isn't their gracious hospitality.'

There was a silence while this information sank in. Then Conchita started crying again.

'Did you have to mention that?' complained Frank. 'Now you've gone and upset her all over again.'

'We noticed,' said Ethan dismally.

At that moment Tlaloc strode across and urged them to their feet. 'We go,' he said – so there were at least two other words of English that he knew.

Ethan got to his feet and Stetson came over and grabbed the rope around his neck. He gave it a yank and whistled, as if to a dog, then laughed at the American's angry reaction. He said something in that strange sing-song language and set off, dragging Ethan behind him. The others had no option but to follow, trudging on through the rising heat of the day.

CHAPTER ELEVEN

Jungle Boy

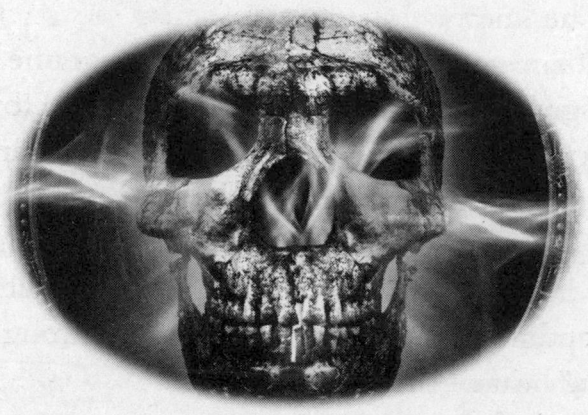

Alec moved higher and higher into the canopy of the tree, hugging the branches close to his chest and praying that he didn't lose his footing on the slippery bark. He was already some thirty feet up, but he realized he needed to be much higher to see over the tops of the other trees. He reached out a hand to pull himself up to the next branch, then froze as he heard a sound just ahead of him.

He caught a glimpse of a pair of yellow eyes and a mouth fringed with sharp yellow teeth. Then a deep rumbling growl turned the blood in his veins to ice. The creature came into focus. Its spotted hide had merged so perfectly with the patterns of dappled light around it that Alec had been completely unaware of its presence until he was almost on top of it. A jaguar was stretched out on a branch and had just registered his approach. As Alec watched, transfixed, the big cat came up into a crouch, its claws tearing strips out of the stout limb it had been resting on.

Alec swallowed hard. For a moment he didn't know what to do. He tried to remember whether anybody had ever given him any advice about what to do in such a situation, and decided that the best option would be to run in the opposite direction.

Only he couldn't do that. He was thirty feet up; a fall from this height would almost certainly kill him. He began to lower his outstretched arm, gritting his teeth as he did so, but the jaguar immediately gave a roar that nearly knocked him backwards out of the tree.

'Here, kitty, kitty!' Alec heard himself utter the words and thought he had never said anything so stupid in his entire life. The jaguar retreated a few steps, its tail coiling agitatedly behind it. It seemed to be deliberating whether or not to attack.

Alec snatched a breath and began to lower his foot to the branch below. The movement seemed to infuriate the big cat. It roared again, the volume ear-shattering at such close range; panicked by the noise, Alec tried to move his other foot down but found himself stepping into empty air: he was falling! He threw out a hand and tried to grab at a branch, but it was rotten and collapsed beneath his fingers like powder.

He fell backwards, staring up at the jaguar, which was climbing down after him. He winced at the thought of hitting the ground, but the impact came sooner than he'd expected: he crashed into a branch and let out a yell of surprise, and then into another, and another, and then another, his entire body jolted – though he was so full of adrenalin, he barely registered the pain. As he fell, Alec tried to grab handfuls of leaves – and suddenly, miraculously, his fingers found a grip, and his downward impetus was halted so suddenly that his arm was nearly pulled out of its socket. He hung there for a moment, stunned. Then, looking down, he saw that he was perhaps eight feet above the ground.

There was a crack, and the branch Alec was holding broke off. He dropped again, but was now falling feet first. He remembered how Mr Goodwin, the PT instructor at his last school, always used to tell him to bend his knees and roll forward, and he automatically did exactly that. His feet thudded into the soft ground and he went into a forward roll and came upright with a shout of triumph; but the growl behind him was a grim reminder that his ordeal was not yet over.

Alec turned round and saw the lithe spotted shape of the jaguar coming down the tree in a series of agile bounds and reminded himself that this was the point where he was supposed to run. For a moment his legs seemed to have seized up and he almost collapsed.

But terror lent him strength and he put down his head and started to sprint, not even sure where he was running. The shadowy opening of a narrow trail appeared ahead of him and he threw himself along it, knowing that he could not outrun the cat for long. He glanced back over his shoulder to see the jaguar coming after him, as silent as a ghost, narrowing the gap between them by the second. Alec was just telling himself that he'd have to stop and fight it off when, quite suddenly, the trail ended and he went flying, his arms and legs flailing wildly. He landed on his backside in the mud and began to slide downhill, twisting and turning as he went, completely out of control. The first drop ended in another, steeper drop and he hurtled through the air. He seemed to fall for a long time. Then, unexpectedly, he crashed headlong into a man, knocking him to the ground. Alec rolled over a couple more times and lay there, dizzy and disorientated. He shook his head, sat up and saw that a whole bunch of people were staring down at him in complete surprise. He recognized Ethan and Coates and the others. Then he saw that the man he had collided with was Stetson, the Indian who had stolen Ethan's hat. His companions were laughing delightedly at the bewildered expression on his face.

Ethan, astounded by Alec's sudden appearance, tried to make a move, but half a dozen spear points were pressed to his chest before he could take so much as a step. He scowled and looked down at Alec.

'Kid, that was about the bravest thing I ever saw!' he said; and Alec began to laugh – just a chuckle at first, but then hysterically as he realized the full significance of what had just happened. They thought he had just launched a rescue attempt. He glanced back and pointed up the incline, trying to find the words to explain.

'I was . . . up a tree!' he jabbered. 'There was a . . . a—'

'Master Alec, whatever's come over you?' asked Coates, which only made Alec laugh all the harder. Then the Indians helped Stetson to his feet and approached Alec holding lengths of twine. He tried to struggle to his feet, but then Stetson slapped him hard across his face. Before he knew it, he was down on the ground and his wrists were being secured behind his back, just like the others.

Some rescue attempt, he thought bitterly, and then he was yanked upright, tied in place in front of Ethan, and Stetson was yanking hard on the rope around his neck, a smile of grim pleasure on his face.

'Nice try, kid,' said Ethan.

Alec just shrugged his shoulders, too exhausted after his ordeal to explain exactly what had happened. Stetson pulled on the rope and he could do nothing but follow him.

★ ★ ★

All through the afternoon they walked along narrow overgrown trails where ferns and vines hung in their faces. Alec's shirt was sodden with sweat and his wrists rubbed raw by the tight bonds. He was aching in a dozen places where he had hit branches in his fall and would have given anything to stop for a rest, but whenever he tried speaking to Tlaloc, the warning glare he received was enough to make him shut up again. He was just beginning to wonder if he could possibly walk another step when the Indians turned onto a wider, clearly defined trail that led straight ahead into the forest; the dense vegetation on either side had evidently been cut back.

On either side of them the jungle gradually thinned out. Tlaloc spoke to one of his warriors and the man nodded and sprinted off, presumably to give notice of their arrival. Alec saw an ancient stone archway ahead of them, carved with depictions of Aztec gods. He recognized the maize goddess, Chicomecoatl, and Xipe Totec, the god of the spring; but at the very centre of the arch a hideous skull-like face grinned down at the approaching party. Alec felt a sense of dread, for he knew that this was the image of Mictlantecuhtli, the god of the dead; and that this position at the centre of the arch announced that the captives were now entering a place that was dedicated to him.

He glanced over his shoulder and saw that Ethan was looking up at the arch with a grim expression on his face. Even if the American didn't recognize the god he was looking at, that awful skull left nobody in any doubt about its meaning.

Beyond the arch, the ground was covered in cobblestones; ahead, a couple of smooth stone steps led up to a higher level. Now Alec could see that there were dwellings on either side of them, simple wattle and daub huts with thatched roofs to begin with; but as they walked on, these were replaced by grander dwellings made of adobe, with elaborate stone roofs. Most of the buildings were based around a central courtyard; there were people walking around – the men mostly naked save for loincloths and the occasional multi-coloured woven cloak, the women in loose-fitting blouses and full-length skirts, their black hair tied into buns. Groups of children ran here and there, squealing and shouting.

Alec was amazed by what he was seeing. Part

of him was terrified by the thought of what might be awaiting them, but he was also fascinated: he seemed to have stepped into a time machine and flown back some six hundred years to an era that should not even exist in the modern age. As he looked around, he saw people engaged in their everyday routines: women cooking on open charcoal fires or grinding maguey cactus into flour; men working on houses, plastering wooden frameworks with handfuls of adobe. Here a woman sat in an open courtyard, weaving a piece of cloth. There, a line of men carried straw baskets of what looked like maize upon their backs. But as the captives were led past, every person stopped to stare at them in silence.

Now they passed a loop of a broad river. Alec could see a wooden jetty and many dugout canoes moored beside it. In the shallows men with spears stood watching for fish; their catch hung from a wooden frame, plump bodies shimmering in the sunlight. On the far side of the river, other men were working in the fields.

The prisoners were led into the heart of the city, the buildings ever more elaborate, until they were passing by dwellings supported by huge stone columns. Then they rounded a corner, and there was the edifice that Alec had spotted from the plane – a huge step pyramid of smooth-plastered stone that rose high into the air. It culminated in a platform, where once again a huge stone figure of Mictlantecuhtli stood behind an altar like a great demon presiding over his empire. There was a look on the statue's skull-like face that seemed to express an unspeakable evil. There was something odd about the pyramid, Alec noticed, something he hadn't seen from the plane. The summit seemed to be hollow and from it issued a haze, as though a great heat was rising from within it.

Around the base of the pyramid, a curious crowd was assembled – mostly men with shoulder-length hair, their faces painted with bright colours or blackened with what looked like soot. Some of them were wailing and one man, stripped to the waist, was sticking cactus needles into his bare flesh, which ran with blood. Others were beating their backs with canes, their eyes staring as though they were in a trance. One old man scampered towards Alec and started performing some kind of mad dance in front of him, but the guards pushed him away and led their prisoners onwards.

Off to the side of the pyramid, on a raised platform, two figures were waiting, as though they had been expecting these guests. The first was a tall thin man wearing an elaborate feathered headdress, a multi-coloured beaded yoke, metal bracelets, and a long cloak decorated with thousands of shimmering green quetzal feathers. He had a cruel face, Alec thought; he was somebody to be feared. He stood there, observing the approaching captives with a sardonic smile, but it was impossible to tell what might be in his mind.

The man beside him was more simply dressed in a white cotton singlet that hung to his knees; he was shorter by a good six inches. He was also much older and had a thick grey beard. Though his skin was darkened by years of exposure to the sun, Alec could see that he was a white man – and as if to confirm the fact, the eyes that surveyed him as he came up the last few steps were pale blue in colour.

There was a silence and they stood there, waiting for somebody to speak. Ethan opened his mouth to say something but the old man lifted a hand to stop him. He smiled.

'Good day to you,' he said, in a cultured voice that was unmistakably English. 'May I welcome you to the city of Colotlán, which in your tongue means . . . the place of scorpions.'

CHAPTER TWELVE

Travers

There was another long silence after that. Alec stood there staring at the old man: he had so many questions forming in his head, he hardly knew which one to ask first. At last he came up with something that sounded about as stupid as was humanly possible.

'You're an Englishman!'

But the bearded man shook his head. 'No,' he said, 'I *was* an Englishman once, long ago, when I was . . . young and foolish. Now I am Aztec.' He spoke in a slow, halting manner, as though he had to think carefully about every word before uttering it. 'You must . . . ah . . . forgive me. I have not had much occasion to use my . . . my native tongue, except to teach some of the people here the . . . the occasional phrase. It amuses them.'

Ethan shot a look at Tlaloc. 'Yeah, I think you taught laughing boy there just four words. *Shut up* and *We go*!'

The old man chuckled at this. 'That would be . . . about right,' he admitted. 'I have two . . . students, who have learned very well, but most are content with the odd word. Forgive me . . . my name – my *Aztec* name – is Coyotl, which in your tongue means wolf. The people here think of me as' – he had to consider for a moment – 'cunning! Yes, that's the word. They think of the coyote as a cunning creature and some thought I had that . . . that quality about me. But of course, back in the days when I . . . lived among the white men, I had another name. Travers.'

Nelson seemed to recognize this. '*Colonel* Travers?' he murmured. 'Colonel William Travers?'

Travers bowed his head. 'Ah, I see somebody has . . . heard of me!' he said.

'I should say I have! A big story once, though I guess I'm going back fifteen, twenty years?' He looked around at the others. 'None of you ever heard of Colonel Travers? An unsolved mystery around Veracruz,' he explained. 'It was in all the papers. The colonel here headed up an expedition into the Huasteca Veracruzana back in . . . what – must have been nineteen ten or thereabouts? His team set off into the jungle and were never heard of again. People at my oil rigs still talk about it to this day. You're a legend, Colonel Travers.'

'Really?' Travers looked genuinely surprised. 'I must say I'm . . . astonished to learn this. It was a very long time ago.'

'Well, you don't know how glad we are to meet you,' said Frank.

'I am . . . delighted to hear it,' said Travers. 'Though how long your delight will last is . . . debatable. Yes, I believe that's the word. Debatable.' He seemed to remember the man standing beside him and bowed his head politely. 'This man is called Itztli,' he said. 'He's the . . . high priest of the temple of Mictlantecuhtli; next to the emperor he's possibly the most . . . powerful man in this city.'

Everybody bowed their heads to Itztli but he seemed unmoved. Alec had a bad feeling about him. He'd had dealings with a high priest once before . . .

Itztli looked at Travers and said something to him. The colonel nodded and turned back to face them.

'Itztli asks about the . . . er . . . sky chariot you came in,' he said. 'I told him it's only a . . . a machine that men have made, much like the biplanes I remember from my days in the military. But he demands to know what . . . magic makes it fly.'

Ethan laughed at that. 'Tell him the magic's all gone. Damned thing crashed and went up in flames. We were lucky to survive.'

Travers conveyed this information and Itztli considered it for a moment. Then he spoke quickly and agitatedly. Travers nodded and conveyed the message.

'Itztli says that Quetzalcoatl, the god of the air, tore you from the sky for . . . daring to trespass in his domain.'

'Yeah, whatever,' said Ethan. 'Listen, pal, do you think you could get these boys to cut through our ties? I'm starting to lose the feeling in my hands.'

Travers looked at him blankly. 'Why . . . Why would I do that?' he asked.

Ethan stared at him. 'Why? Because you're an

Englishman and there's three English people in this party. And two Americans. Don't forget, we fought beside you in the Great War!'

'There was a war?' asked Travers.

'Heck, yes, the Great War. The war to end all wars. That's what they called it. It was us versus Germany.'

'*Us?*' Travers looked uncomfortable with this description. 'I cannot say I am surprised,' he said. 'I thought a war was coming – that is why I . . . came to Mexico in the first place. I'd had enough of the modern world. I came into the Huasteca Veracruzana looking . . . for adventure. After months of searching, I and my companions found this.' He gestured around at the city. 'Can you wonder that I elected to stay? Look at it, my friends! Is it not . . . incredible?'

'It is,' admitted Alec. 'All of it. It looks as though it hasn't changed for hundreds of years. It . . . it's like stepping into a time machine.' He gazed up. 'Can I ask, though . . .'

'Yes?' murmured Travers.

'The heat rising from the step pyramid – what is that exactly?'

Travers followed his gaze as though he hadn't noticed before. Then he turned back and smiled.

'The temple is built over the gateway . . . to the underworld,' he said.

Alec stared at him, puzzled. 'You mean . . . it's built over an active volcano?'

Travers shook his head. 'I mean what I said. The words you use are those a white man would say. But every person in this city knows that . . . below us lies the land of Mictlan – the underworld. That is why this city was built here and . . . dedicated to the god who rules that world.'

Alec frowned. 'But . . . isn't that incredibly dangerous? I mean, what if the volcano were to erupt? It could destroy everything.'

Travers smiled. 'You do not understand,' he said. 'Provided we continue to . . . appease the god, that will not happen. We have always been at Mictlantecuhtli's mercy. Oh, he has shaken his fist at us many times over the years. He has caused damage, for sure. But he is merciful. If we obey his laws and make the necessary . . . sacrifices to him, we will continue to receive his mercy.'

Coates snorted in disbelief. 'Oh, come along now, you can't believe that mumbo jumbo! You're a civilized man, for goodness' sake.'

Travers looked at the valet and his expression became cold and hard. 'You are ignorant of our ways, so I will . . . overlook your words this time. Be sure that Itztli does not learn that you have uttered such . . . blasphemy, for he would not be so forgiving.' He looked around at the dismayed faces. 'And please do not think that I cling to any of my old beliefs. I still have the language, but I am Aztec now. I follow their ways, *their* beliefs.'

Ethan shrugged his shoulders. 'Well, we're all real pleased for you, Colonel. But listen, if you'd just cut us free and point us in the right direction, we'll be out of your hair and you can get on with whatever it is you guys do for fun around here.'

Travers stared at Ethan for a moment, then threw back his head and laughed. He said something to Itztli and the priest laughed too, but it was a cold, mirthless laugh.

Alec and Ethan exchanged baffled looks.

'Listen,' said the American. 'Maybe I'm missing something here, but I wasn't aware that I had such a gift for comedy.'

Travers sighed. 'You are going nowhere, my friend. You are our . . . guests and you will be staying with us until we decide what is to be done with you.'

At this, Conchita pushed her way forward.

'You don' understand,' she told Travers. 'I can't stay here. I have a screen test in Tonala with Louis B. Mayer.'

Travers stared at her, as though she was speaking a completely different language. Itztli too was gazing at her with interest. He said something to the old man, looking at Conchita all the time. Travers nodded.

'The high priest says that you are very . . . beautiful,' he told Conchita.

'Tell him thanks a bunch, but I need to get out of this dump.'

Alec winced. Probably not the most diplomatic thing to say about the Aztec city, he thought.

'It is *you* who do not understand,' Travers explained. 'You have found favour with Itztli. He honours you by offering to . . . give you to the emperor as one of his wives.'

'As one of his . . .' Conchita stared at the high priest, her mouth open in dismay. 'Ay-yi-yi. But . . . I can't do that, I already have a husban'.' She jerked her head at Frank. 'This my husban',' she said desperately. 'He won' like it if I marry somebody else — isn't that so, Frank?'

'Er . . . yeah, that's right,' agreed Frank, going

along with her. 'We . . . we been married for years, ain't we? You can't just take somebody cos you like the look of her! That ain't cricket!'

Travers spoke to Itztli and the priest shrugged his shoulders, as though he'd been told something of no consequence. He gestured to Tlaloc and said something to him in Nahuatl. The warrior strode forward, pulling a huge knife from his belt. Frank stared at him, his eyes bulging in terror, but Tlaloc simply cut through the ropes binding him and Conchita together. He took her roughly by the shoulder and started to lead her away. Frank tried to follow, but with his hands tied behind his back there was really nothing he could do.

'Take your hands off of her!' he bellowed. 'How *dare* you!'

Tlaloc simply raised a hand and slapped the Englishman hard across the face, knocking him back into the others. He stumbled and nearly fell but Luis and Nelson helped him regain his feet. Tlaloc summoned a couple of his warriors, who ran forward and began to drag Conchita away. She struggled and shouted as she was propelled through an open doorway in a stone building that adjoined the temple.

'This is not right!' she shrieked. 'I'm a Mexican citizen! You can't push me around. I don't wanna marry nobody! Frank! Frank, help me!'

They could hear her voice echoing as she was led away down unseen corridors.

Frank spun round, glaring at Travers. 'You can't do this!' he yelled. 'Call yourself a gentleman? You're acting more like a ruddy savage!'

Travers seemed unconcerned by Frank's outburst. 'I do not call myself . . . a gentleman. And if you see me as a savage, then so be it. I have told you, I am Aztec now. And here in this city, Itztli's word is law. I would advise you to keep quiet.'

'I will not stay quiet!' roared Frank. 'You can't push us around like this. I—'

'Frank, pipe down!' snapped Ethan irritably. 'Shouting isn't going to change anything. Don't worry, we'll figure something out.' He stared at Travers. 'OK, Colonel,' he said. 'Mind telling us what happens next?'

Travers spread his hands in a gesture of helplessness. 'For now, you will be kept in a . . . a secure place. Itztli wishes to speak to the lord of Mictlan and seek his guidance in this matter.'

'Oh yeah, how does that work? He's gonna get him on the telephone, is he?'

Travers looked at Ethan for a moment, then said something to Tlaloc, who stepped forward and punched Ethan in the stomach. The big man doubled up, forcing Alec down too.

'Ethan,' he gasped. 'Are you all right?'

He nodded. Rage blazed in his eyes but with his hands tied behind his back he was powerless to do anything. He glared up at Tlaloc.

Travers regarded him calmly. 'Allow me to explain how this works,' he said. 'When I first came here all those years ago, with the . . . the other members of my expedition, we were . . . taken prisoner, just as you are. Many of my companions could not accept that they were . . . slaves and tried to fight against it. I watched them die. Many of them died badly, screaming for mercy. But from my very first glimpse of Colotlán, I knew I wanted to belong to it. I gave myself up to my captors and I . . . undertook all the trials of strength they made me submit to. I came close to dying . . . many times, but in the end, I . . . I . . . convinced them that I was of good heart, that I wanted to be like them. It takes great . . . courage to be an Aztec, my friends. Courage and strength. Some of you may have those qualities within you. Those who do not will go to meet the lord of the underworld.'

Alec considered these words and felt a cold dread rising within him. He knew all about the blood sacrifices made by the Aztecs and he knew also that being just a boy would not exempt him from death. Children were often sacrificed too.

'Get up now,' Travers told them. 'Tonight you rest, and perhaps with the morning will come news of your fate.'

Ethan and Alec struggled to their feet. Ethan glared at the old man. 'Just so you know,' he said. 'You just made it onto my list of people that I don't much care for.'

Travers shrugged. 'Ah well,' he said. 'I suppose I'll just have to . . . live with that.' He lifted a hand to summon Tlaloc, but as he did so, Alec felt a strange tremor in the stone beneath his boots. It started gently but then started shaking in earnest, threatening to topple him off his feet. Then he heard a deep rumble far below. There was an abrupt whoosh of air and he looked up at the summit of the pyramid, just in time to see a flash of light and a great cloud of black smoke belching out from the flue and darkening the sky above them.

Itztli turned to look at it too, an expression of delight on his thin face.

The tremor lasted only a few moments. Then it subsided and the ground was still again. The high priest turned back to look at the remaining warriors from the hunting party, who seemed to be waiting for his words. He said something in Nahuatl – something that sounded jubilant – and the men cheered and raised their fists in the air.

Travers smiled at the captives. 'Itztli says this is a good omen,' he said. 'The lord of the underworld expresses his . . . pleasure at the arrival of the outsiders.'

Ethan looked at him in disgust. 'You're as crazy as a bed bug,' he said.

The colonel seemed to have no answer to that. He signalled to the warriors and they took hold of their prisoners and began to herd them towards the building into which Conchita had been taken.

'This is not good,' said Coates dismally as they were propelled along cool stone corridors. 'This is not good at all.'

And for once in his life, Alec was in total agreement.

CHAPTER THIRTEEN

In Limbo

They were pushed into a small chamber, which unlike most of the other rooms through which they had passed had a solid metal door. Glancing around quickly, Alec could see that there were no windows, just white plastered stone walls. Light came in through a square opening in the ceiling above them, but this was criss-crossed by a series of stout wooden beams; a grille that was too narrow to squeeze through. Wooden bunks with woven mattresses stood along one wall, and up at the far end there was a small open latrine. Half a dozen guards entered the room with them and stood guard as Tlaloc took out his knife and cut through their bonds. Alec gave a sigh of relief and rubbed his wrists, feeling the blood flowing back into them.

'That's a relief,' he said.

Ethan nodded. He too was looking around, clearly seeking some avenue of escape, but it seemed hopeless. The opening in the ceiling offered the only possible way out, but as Alec gazed up, he saw the impassive face of a guard looking down at him and realized that the Aztecs had it covered.

'What happens now?' asked Nelson, but nobody had an answer.

Travers appeared in the doorway and stood there, smiling. 'Make yourselves comfortable,' he told them. 'For tonight, at least, you are our guests. I will arrange for food and water to be brought to you. Tomorrow you will be taken to meet Chicahua, our emperor. He will decide what is to happen to you.'

Coates frowned. 'Why do I get the impression that's not going to be the most pleasant of out-comes?' he asked.

'You must take heart, my friend,' the old man said. 'When I was first brought here, I had the worst . . . expectations. But here I am, alive and well.'

Luis stepped forward. 'Listen,' he said. 'I'm to blame for us being here. You can do whatever you want to me, but I ask you to spare the lives of these others.'

Travers seemed amused by this. 'It is not for me to decide your fate,' he told him. 'I want you to know that I personally wish you no harm.'

'I'll bet Itztli doesn't feel that way,' said Alec bitterly.

Travers shrugged. 'Itztli carries out the bidding of Mictlantecuhtli,' he said. 'And if the lord of the dead asks for you to join him, you will be sent down to the underworld. Though even the high priest must bow to the wishes of his emperor.'

'Then we'd do well to make a good impression,' observed Coates. 'I wonder if perhaps you could arrange to have my clothes cleaned and pressed?'

Travers laughed at that. 'You are an amusing fellow,' he said. 'Let us hope you can keep your sense of humour. It may be sorely tested in the days to come.'

Meanwhile Frank was pacing agitatedly around the room, glaring at Travers and the guards. 'What have you done with Conchita?' he demanded to know.

Travers raised his eyebrows. 'Conchita? Ah, the woman! You need have no worries about her. Itztli will present her to the emperor: she will be kept in comfort and no harm shall befall her, I can assure you of that. Unless of course she displeases her new husband.'

'You tell him if he so much as lays a finger on her, he'll have me to answer to.'

Travers sighed. 'I shall do no such thing,' he said. 'You would be better advised to watch your tongue and worry about your own fate, my friend. Your Conchita will have a life of pampered comfort. You, on the other hand, may have only a few hours left. Use them wisely.'

He left them and disappeared along the corridor. The guards backed towards the doorway. Tlaloc went out last, watching them all intently.

'Food come soon,' he told them; and then the door slammed and they heard the sound of bolts being slid into position.

They all stood there, looking hopelessly at each other. Then Ethan sighed and went and sat down on one of the bunks.

'What are you doing?' Nelson wanted to know.

'Getting some rest until the food arrives,' said Ethan.

Nelson stared at him incredulously. 'How can you think of resting?' he cried. 'These savages intend to kill us!'

'We don't actually know that yet,' Alec told him. 'Maybe this emperor will decide to keep us alive.'

'Yeah, dream on, kid,' snarled Nelson. 'Maybe he'll throw a big party for us, with Jell-O and ice cream! We should be looking for a way out of here.'

'Be my guest,' said Coates, taking a seat on another bunk. 'Does anybody mind if I take my shoes off? My feet are killing me.'

Nobody objected so he unlaced his heavy boots and pulled off his socks. He stared down at his feet. 'I do believe I've got blisters!'

'You are incredible!' Nelson turned to Frank, thinking perhaps that he might have more luck with him. 'Don't you think we should be doing something?' he asked.

Frank just looked miserable. 'I can't stop thinkin' about Conchita,' he said. 'She must be terrified.'

'The hell with Conchita! *I'm* terrified. I

can't believe you're all just sitting around here!'

'What would you have us do?' asked Luis. 'Señor Wade is right, there's nothing we can achieve right now. We may as well just try and get some rest.'

'You stay out of this, Chavez! You've forfeited your right to have any say in what goes on here. I tell you this: if we ever make it back to civilization, I'm going to see to it that you pay for your crimes. I'll be there laughing when they sentence you to twenty years in a stinking jail.'

Coates was massaging one of his feet. 'I had some very good ointment in my pack,' he murmured. 'It would have taken care of these blisters very effectively. I suppose one of those Aztecs has it now.'

'Maybe we could ask for a bowl of hot water when they come back,' suggested Alec, sitting down beside Coates. 'And some salt. I suppose they have salt? I believe that's a good treatment for blisters.'

'My pa always swore by rubbing alcohol,' said Ethan. 'Always seemed to do the trick. Hey, if we get to talk to Travers again, maybe he could find out what happened to your ointment?'

Nelson stared at them for a moment, then

shook his head. He went along to the furthest bunk and threw himself down on it, his face turned away. Luis also climbed up into the bunk above Ethan. Only Frank remained on his feet, walking up and down agitatedly and staring at the solid metal door.

'I hope Conchita's all right,' he said hopelessly. 'I hope they haven't hurt her.'

Conchita lay in the deep stone bath, up to her neck in deliciously hot water perfumed with aromatic flower petals. A group of young Indian women attended her, some bringing in large gold jugs containing more hot water to top up the bath, others laying out a selection of clothes for her to try when she was ready.

It was only just beginning to dawn on her that nobody here seemed to want to harm her. On the contrary, the girls had been welcoming – giggling and talking excitedly amongst themselves, as though her arrival was the most amazing thing that had ever happened. The moment the guards had pushed her into the chamber, they had cut through her bonds and massaged her sore wrists. Meanwhile, the bath had been filled, and when it was ready, she had been helped to undress – her pleas for a little privacy ignored.

One woman who was older than the others knew a few words of English and had identified herself as Nelli. She was plump and pleasant-looking with huge brown eyes, her hair braided and pinned up on top of her head. She wore a plain white dress and some exotic-looking pieces of jewellery. She stayed beside the bath, talking to Conchita while the other girls moved to and fro around her.

'You lucky,' she said now, smiling down at her. 'You wife of emperor, you stay here with us.'

Conchita frowned up at her. 'I can't stay here long,' she said. 'I have a screen test.'

Nelli smiled. It was evident she didn't have a clue what this meant. 'You *stay*. Very nice here. Good food, all you want!' She patted her ample tummy. 'You need flesh on bones, like Nelli.'

'But . . . I don't want to marry this . . . emperor.'

Nelli made a dismissive gesture with her hand, as though it was of little consequence. 'It is decided,' she told Conchita. 'Chicahua take you as wife, but there is no need to worry. You will understand when you meet him.'

She said something in Nahuatl to the other girls and they fell into a fit of giggling. Nelli lifted a finger to her lips to shush them. 'Come,' she said. 'You clean now. Ready for food.'

This reminded Conchita that she hadn't eaten a thing since the previous night. She got out of the bath and a couple of women hurried forward to hold up a woven cotton towel to preserve her modesty. She felt embarrassed, but before she could say anything, two more girls were towelling her dry, giving her the kind of attention they might give to a baby.

'I'll do that,' she kept saying, but they ignored her protests, smiling up at her in apparent devotion. It occurred to her that they were treating her almost like a celebrity. This must be what it was like to be a star of motion pictures.

A selection of clothes were brought to her, from which she chose a loose-fitting cotton dress. Before she knew it she was seated on a kind of throne with women braiding her hair and clasping beautiful jewellery around her wrists and neck. A polished metal mirror was held up so she could see her reflection. She was frankly astonished. With her hair done like this and dressed in the unfamiliar clothes, she could easily have passed for an Aztec woman.

'You like *us* now,' said Nelli, guessing at her thoughts.

Conchita allowed herself a smile, but her empty stomach was complaining and she reminded the other woman about her promise of food.

'Ah, yes!' Nelli clapped her hands and more girls hurried into the room carrying platters containing a bewildering variety of foods. Conchita recognized corn pancakes filled with red beans and tomatoes, and pieces of cold fish wrapped in fragrant leaves. There were also large chunks of succulent meat that she could not identify but tasted delicious. She was handed a clay bowl and encouraged to take what she wanted. There was no cutlery of any kind, so she ate with her fingers, pushing handfuls of food into her mouth. One platter held an assortment of what looked like large fried grasshoppers. She kept waving it away, until Nelli, thinking she was being overly polite, picked up the biggest and crammed it into her mouth. Terrified of offending anyone, Conchita made herself take one; it was horribly crunchy but tasted of chicken. A clay goblet of brown liquid was handed to her, and she was astonished to discover that it was thick, sweet drinking chocolate. She took a mouthful and the women all laughed and pointed at her. One of them held out the mirror and she saw she had a dark moustache across her top lip. She laughed too and wiped it away with the back of her hand. She reached for one last chunk of meat and then hesitated, holding it out to Nelli with a questioning look on her face.

'Pig?' she asked.

Nelli smiled, shook her head.

'Chicken?'

The woman looked baffled, clearly not recognizing the word, so Conchita made a clucking sound and waggled her folded arms like wings. Nelli caught on and shook her head again, laughing. She thought for a moment, but couldn't come up with the word, so she made a barking sound.

Conchita let the piece of meat fall from her fingers. She stared at Nelli in absolute horror. 'Dog?' she whispered.

Nelli grinned and nodded. 'Dog!' she said delightedly. 'Good, yes?'

Conchita could feel the colour draining from her face; she stopped eating after that. She was thinking of Pepe, her little poodle back home in Acapulco, and it was all she could do to stop herself from throwing up.

Itztli made his way into the heart of the pyramid and descended the narrow stone staircase that led down into its bowels. Along the walls, rows of lanterns sent out a flickering light. Tlaloc followed him, staying a respectful distance behind. Few people ever came down here, and only the high priest ever took the winding stairs to the very end.

They came to an ancient golden doorway and Itztli glanced at Tlaloc, who turned his back. The door had an intricate locking system – a series of buttons and levers that had to be pressed in a certain order – and Itztli always insisted that nobody else should witness how he did it. This was his secret, only to be passed on to the man who would inherit his powers when he was old and failing. The high priest had recently taken to bringing Tlaloc along with him, telling him that he feared enemies might be lying in wait for him in these dark corridors. But the truth was, he had other plans for the warrior in the not-too-distant future and needed to get him used to the idea of coming down here regularly.

The door mechanism gave a dull clunk as the lock opened. He pushed the heavy door open, aware as he did so of the incredible heat radiating from within. He took a burning torch from the wall beside him and went inside, closing the door behind him. Ahead, the heat rose up from the great open wound in the earth that led down to the realm of Mictlan. He descended the final flight of steps to the gallery; as he drew nearer, the torch became unnecessary, the scene lit by the fiery red glow.

Itztli never failed to be humbled and amazed by what lay before him. Somewhere back in history, at the very beginnings of his race, some-body must have discovered this place and recognized it as a passage to the home of a god. They had first created this great gallery, a circular pathway centred around and above the gateway to Mictlan. Later, they had built a temple above it, a simple stone building with a central opening through which the fumes and heat of Mictlan could be released. In time, over the years, another temple had been built over the first one, bigger and more elaborate. Over the centuries, more layers had been added, each covering the one beneath, until finally the giant step pyramid reared like a colossus above everything. But deep at its core, the great wound remained open; and through each successive layer, the flue that allowed Mictlantecuhtli's power to vent itself into the sky was left open.

Itztli leaned out over the chest-high wall and stared down into the void, feeling the raw heat of the molten rock on his face; and he called out to Mictlantecuhtli, not aloud, but allowing the voice in his head to speak for him, as he had learned to do over the years.

Awake, Great Lord, his inner voice screamed. *It is I, your humble servant, who call you. Awaken and grant me the honour of speaking to me.*

There was a long silence then and he began to think that the god did not have ears to listen to him today. But then, far, far below in the very bowels of the earth, there was a rumbling sound and suddenly the god's voice sounded in his head, a voice like no other – a strange hiss of scalding air and bubbling lava; but Itztli knew how to interpret the words only too well.

ITZTLI, WHAT BRINGS YOU TO ME?

I have them in my power, Great Lord. The outsiders, the ones who dared to defile your ceremony.

AH, GOOOOOD!

I come only to ask what you would have me do with them, Great One.

SEND THEM TO ME, ITZTLI. RELEASE THEIR SOULS WITH YOUR OBSIDIAN BLADE AND SEND THEM TO STAND BESIDE ME IN MICTLAN.

You would not choose to spare them, as you did Coyotl?

COYOTL CAME TO OUR CITY ON FOOT, ITZTLI. HE WAS MEEK AND HUMBLE AND HE SUBMITTED HIMSELF TO ALL OUR INVESTIGATIONS, ALL OUR CEREMONIES. HE PROVED HIMSELF WORTHY AND I WAS WILLING TO PARDON HIM. BUT THESE BLASPHEMERS IN THEIR SKY CHARIOT, THEY HAD TO BE CAUGHT AND DRAGGED HERE IN CHAINS. THERE SHALL BE NO SUCH MERCY FOR THEM. I WANT THEM HERE, WHERE THEY CAN FEEL THE FULL WRATH OF MY POWERS.

I shall deliver them to you, my lord. Only . . .

ONLY WHAT?

Tomorrow they must first meet with Chicahua.

AND?

Chicahua worries me, my lord. He is just a stupid boy.

AND YOUR EMPEROR, ITZTLI. DON'T FORGET THAT!

Yes, but I worry he will not do the right thing by you. You know how fanciful he is. How . . . weak. He may decide to spare the outsiders. And I . . . I cannot go against his word: he is the emperor.

A long silence. Mictlantecuhtli seemed to be deliberating. Itztli waited, hardly daring to breathe.

AS YOU SAY, ITZTLI, HE IS BUT A BOY. EVERYBODY KNOWS THAT YOU ARE THE MOST POWERFUL MAN IN THE CITY. PERHAPS IT IS TIME YOU LISTENED TO WHAT THE OTHER PRIESTS HAVE TOLD YOU. PERHAPS IT IS TIME YOU SEIZED POWER FOR YOURSELF.

Itztli nodded and licked his dry lips. The heat of the molten rock far below drew out large drops of sweat on his face and his gown was sticking to his skinny body.

My lord . . . if I might be so bold as to ask for your help . . .

There was a dull rumble of thunder below him and Itztli felt the walkway tremble beneath his feet.

YOU DARE TO ASK FOR MY ASSISTANCE?

My lord, only so that I may better serve you — if you would send the children of Mictlan to aid me, then perhaps I could take power . . .

The rumbling settled down again. There was another long silence. Then:

I WILL THINK ON IT, ITZTLI. TAKE THEM TO CHICAHUA. SEE WHAT HE DECIDES. AND SHOULD HE MAKE THE WRONG DECISION . . .

Yes, my lord?

COME AND SPEAK WITH ME AGAIN.

I will.

Itztli waited, staring down at the shifting orange light below, waiting for more words. But nothing came. He forced himself to turn away and retraced his steps along the gallery to the ancient doorway, two red spots dancing in front of his eyes.

He climbed the narrow steps to the door and unlocked it. He stepped through, closing it behind him with an echoing clang. He returned the flaming torch to its place on the wall and walked slowly back to where Tlaloc awaited him. At the sound of the high priest's tread, the warrior turned and regarded him, his face impassive, as though he had no interest in what went on beyond the golden door. Itztli knew he itched to know the truth but was not so stupid as to let his expression betray his curiosity.

'Lead the way,' he ordered.

Tlaloc nodded and, turning, began to climb the steps. Itztli followed him, aware of the sweat cooling on his face.

CHAPTER FOURTEEN

The Gift

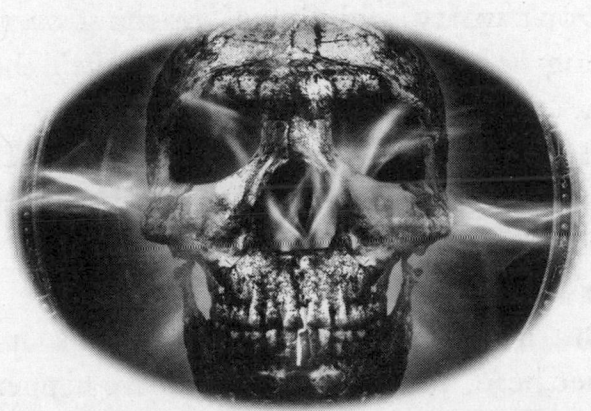

The following morning Alec woke to the sounds of strange discordant music coming from outside their cell. He sat up on his bunk and found that the others were already awake. Coates was listening intently, as though trying to figure something out.

'What is it?' Alec asked him.

'I think it's what passes for music around here. Mostly drums and ocarinas. And I think that nasal sound is what's called a pan pipe.' Coates looked at Alec and smiled reassuringly. 'Whatever it is, it's not going to give Sibelius any sleepless nights.'

Alec tried to smile back but couldn't quite manage it. He was scared and he didn't care who knew it.

'Don't worry,' said Coates, reaching over and putting a hand on his shoulder. 'We'll be all right.'

'How can you say that?' Alec asked him. 'These people are planning to kill us. And . . . besides, it's all my fault.'

'It's nobody's fault.'

'But if I hadn't taken us off to look at that Olmec head, none of this would have happened.'

Coates sighed and shook his head. 'Master Alec, we can spend a lifetime regretting the things we do, but in the end it doesn't make a jot of difference. You have to be positive. Think for a moment: us going on that trip led us here. We're the only white men, apart from Colonel Travers, who have ever seen this place. An Aztec city, unchanged for hundreds of years! In many ways we've been very privileged.'

'Oh yes, we're lucky,' said Alec bitterly. 'But what good is it if we don't live to tell anyone about it?'

'Don't worry, kid,' said Ethan, who was sitting up on the next bunk. 'We won't go without putting up a good fight; and if there's a way out of this mess, we'll find it.'

At that moment they heard footsteps outside and then the noise of bolts being withdrawn. They all looked anxiously towards the door as it swung open. Tlaloc marched in, followed by half a dozen guards, all carrying spears. They formed a formidable-looking line on either side of the door. Then, after a few moments, Travers entered. He was wearing an opulent embroidered cloak and a necklace made of shells and feathers.

'Good morning,' he said. 'I trust you all slept well?'

'How do you suppose we slept?' snarled Nelson. 'It's difficult to relax when you know it might be your last night on earth.'

Travers bowed his head. 'I . . . sympathize,' he said. 'But let's not jump to conclusions. I have come to tell you that his magnificence, the Emperor Chicahua, is ready to receive you. As I told you yesterday, it is he who will make the final decision as to your fate.' He looked around at them. 'I have decided that you should be allowed to walk into his glorious presence with your hands untied. But it would be . . . foolish to think about trying to escape.' He gestured towards the waiting warriors. 'These men have been instructed to kill anyone who tries to run. I have seen them practising with their spears. They never miss.' He gazed at them to make sure everyone understood. 'Good,' he said. 'Now come, it does not do to keep the emperor waiting. He gets bored very easily.'

Travers turned and strode out of the room and Tlaloc urged the captives onto their feet. 'We go,' he said.

'A man of few words,' observed Coates. He looked at Alec. 'Be brave. Let's show them how Englishmen face danger.'

'And Americans,' added Ethan. He glanced at Luis. 'And Mexicans,' he added, but Luis didn't seem to have anything to say to that.

Surrounded by armed warriors, the group made their way out to meet the emperor.

Conchita strolled out of the Hotel Lazaro into the sunlit town square of Tonala. For some strange reason the screen test was to take place here in front of what looked like the entire populace. Among the eager press of onlookers Conchita could see some of her old school friends, looking on in wide-eyed envy.

Determined to make a good impression, she had chosen a dress of red silk and a wide-brimmed straw hat with a red orchid pinned to it. She descended the marble steps of the hotel, and there was Louis B. Mayer waiting to meet her. He was a handsome older man, his hair greying at the temples, giving him a distinguished air. He wore a linen jacket, jodhpurs and long riding boots of expensive leather, and in one hand he carried a megaphone. As Conchita approached him, she wondered where Frank was, but there was no sign of him. Mr Mayer came forward and took her hand. He touched his lips to it respectfully. 'Miss Velez,' he said, 'I'm so glad we finally have the opportunity to meet.'

She smiled and looked around for Frank, but there was still no sign of him.

'It was good of you to wait for me,' she told the producer. 'You wouldn't believe the trouble I had getting here.'

'Good things are worth waiting for,' he assured her. He pointed at the cameraman, standing a short distance away, dwarfed by the big motion picture camera that stood beside him. 'Everything is in readiness,' he said. 'Now, I've taken the trouble to set up a little scenario, something that will demonstrate your range as an actress. If you're happy to start, I'll give you direction from beside the camera.'

'Of course,' she said. She gave a last glance around for Frank. It felt wrong, him not being here. He was always there for her, no matter what. This should have been *his* moment too. He had worked so hard to make it happen.

But then Mr Louis B. Mayer was talking and she realized she would have to concentrate. This was her big chance, the moment she had waited for most of her life. All she had to do was convince the producer that she was a potential star.

'Now, Miss Velez, here's our story. You're waiting in front of the hotel to meet a man — a man you're in love with. I'm going to tell the cameraman to start rolling and you just react to my words.'

She nodded and adopted the expression of a woman in love — which she interpreted with a wan, doe-eyed look; though in reality she had no idea what it was like to be in love. Ever since her poverty-stricken childhood all she had known was the desire to be a star, to be somebody who stood out from the crowd. There hadn't been a lot of room left for affairs of the heart.

'Action,' said Louis B. Mayer, and continued to talk: 'But though you're in love, Miss Velez, you are also apprehensive. You know that there is a rival for your affections who has sworn to avenge himself on the man you have given your heart to.'

Conchita widened her eyes and placed a hand on her breast. She allowed her breathing to quicken.

'Suddenly a shout comes from the crowd! You hear somebody say there has been a terrible accident!'

Conchita snapped her gaze to the left and lifted a hand to her face.

'Now you hear another sound,' said Louis B. Mayer. 'A strange, menacing sound that you have never heard before!'

Conchita narrowed her eyes and let her expression turn to one of surprise.

'You see something approaching you. Not a man, but something from your darkest nightmares.'

Conchita stared across the town square and the look of fear in her face was not an act . . .

because something inexplicable was happening. The sky above the rooftops behind Mr Mayer was darkening, filled with a mass of boiling, writhing clouds; and within the clouds something was moving; something metallic that flashed like stabs of lightning.

Unaware of what was happening behind him, Louis B. Mayer continued to give direction: 'Yes, that's perfect! Hold that feeling a moment, and . . . your apprehension turns to fear as the thing approaches . . .'

Now Conchita could see that the crowds of people behind the great man were beginning to panic. Some were turning to point at the moving darkness that was descending from the sky. Others were scattering in all directions. She wanted to say something but Mr Mayer's words kept her pinned to the spot.

'It is something unspeakably evil and it wants your very soul. You open your mouth and you give vent to your terror. You scream, Miss Velez. You scream for your very life . . .'

Conchita opened her mouth but no sound emerged. It was as though her throat had seized up. She tried to form a sound until beads of sweat appeared on her forehead. She was aware that

Louis B. Mayer was looking at her with a disappointed expression; but he was unaware of the unspeakable thing in the clouds reaching out a withered hand to take him . . .

'Scream, Miss Velez! *Scream!*'

She tried again, summoning all her strength, opening her mouth wide and—

She was shaken roughly awake by Nelli, who appeared to be in a state of high excitement. 'Come, Conchita,' she said. 'We go. Chicahua waits!'

'What?' Conchita looked blearily around her bedroom. For a moment she didn't know where she was; she was still locked in that disturbing dream. Then it all came back to her: the crash in the jungle; their capture by the Indians. She sat up, clutching the sheet to her, to see a group of laughing Aztec women holding out a selection of clothes for her to choose from.

'Who . . . Who is Chick' – she couldn't pronounce the name – 'Chicken Ha-ha?'

'Chicahua is emperor,' said Nelli. 'Your new husban'. Come, you dress now.'

'Don' we have time for no breakfast?' complained Conchita. 'Some pancakes, maybe?' She gave Nelli a look. 'But no dog, please!'

'No time for eat! You hurry!' Nelli bustled away and the other women closed in, giggling excitedly.

Conchita sighed. Clearly being the wife of an emperor wasn't all about lying around and being spoiled. She pointed to a racy little number in pale blue and the women began to dress her.

They emerged into the sunlight and stood blinking at the crowds of shouting, jeering people that surrounded them. There were more than there had been on their arrival. It seemed the entire population had turned out to greet them.

Alec peered around anxiously – he had never experienced anything like this. Everywhere, a confusion of sights and sounds assaulted his senses. He saw warriors dressed in nothing but loincloths, their bodies decorated with tribal scars, their necks and wrists draped with jewellery. He saw prosperous-looking merchants in richly embroidered robes, their wives walking behind them, many with faces covered, accompanied by slaves holding up straw parasols to shade them from the sun. He saw people with painted faces dancing and singing to the accompaniment of primitive instruments; he saw acrobats standing on each other's shoulders to form impossibly high columns; he saw street vendors offering trays of unidentifiable food, children running in and out in noisy groups — and everyone, *everyone* staring at these visitors as though they were monsters from outer space. The guards herded the captives through the crowd; as they passed by, hands came out to touch their hair, to pinch their flesh, to tug at their strange clothes.

'Quit that!' Alec heard Ethan say, but when he turned to look, they had already moved on.

Ethan gave him a fierce look. 'Don't let 'em spook you, kid,' he growled.

Alec nodded, but his heart was hammering in his chest like a piston.

The guards led them towards the open plaza beneath the dark brooding shape of the step pyramid. Several people were waiting for them on a raised platform at the top of a short flight of steps. Alec recognized Itztli, gazing down at them with undisguised hatred, and beside him Travers, smiling but inscrutable. Just behind them stood several other robed men — more priests, Alec surmised — their faces covered by masks depicting the demonic faces of Aztec gods. Trying to stem his mounting fear, he occupied himself by identifying each of them in turn. The scowling snake-like mask depicted Quetzalcoatl, the feathered serpent, god of knowledge and the wind; he thought the human face with its pierced nose and crown of quetzal feathers was a representation of Xipe Totec, god of vegetation and the springtime. But there were other sinister masks that he simply could not put a name to.

'Looks like they've put on quite a show for us,' growled Ethan, staring around defiantly. 'Like Barnum and Bailey's Circus on a Saturday night.'

'Look!' cried Frank. He was pointing at a group of women. Alec followed his gaze but couldn't understand what he was making a fuss about. 'It's Conchita,' explained Frank, and Alec saw that he was right. Her hair was braided, she wore Aztec clothes and jewellery, but her lovely features were unmistakable. She was staring down at them despairingly.

'If they've harmed one hair on her head, they'll be sorry,' said Frank.

'I wouldn't worry about her,' said Nelson. 'She looks like she's landed on her feet, which is more than can be said for the rest of us!'

'Shut up! Get down,' said Tlaloc, motioning

them down onto their knees at the foot of the steps; when Ethan was a little slow in obeying, he jabbed the end of his spear into the back of Ethan's knee, forcing him down onto the stone with a grunt of pain. He urged the others to follow suit and they quickly did as they were told.

'First chance I get to pop that big gorilla on the nose, I'm gonna take it,' said Ethan quietly.

'I wouldn't try that if I were you,' said Coates, sounding as calm and logical as ever. 'I don't think it would go down at all well.'

'Maybe, but it would make *me* feel a whole lot better,' said Ethan. He turned and winked at Alec. 'You hanging on in there, kid?' he asked.

'I've been better,' admitted Alec.

Everyone lifted their heads as the music swelled suddenly into a cacophonous fanfare. A procession was approaching round the side of the step pyramid. It was led and flanked by powerful-looking armed guards, but at its centre, eight slaves walked two by two, carrying a gilded throne on stout poles across their shoulders. On that throne, wearing a gold embroidered cloak and what looked like a collection of priceless jewels, sat a chubby little boy, perhaps twelve years of age.

The son of the emperor, surmised Alec; and he peered through the attendants to see if the father was following behind. But the boy was accompanied only by a tall girl of perhaps fifteen or sixteen and a wiry, bald man who was leading a fully-grown jaguar on a length of rope. The big cat gazed balefully around, looking as if it might attack somebody at any moment.

The slaves lowered the throne to the ground and moved away. The boy sat there, looking down at the captives with interest. The girl and the bald man stood on either side of him. Now Travers approached them and raised a hand to introduce the boy.

'I give you the great, the omnipotent, the most holy Chicahua, emperor of the great city of Colotlán,' he said.

There was a long silence.

'That little kid?' sneered Nelson. 'You're joking, right?'

Travers came forward and slapped the American hard across his face, rocking him back on his knees. 'You are strangers here,' he snarled, 'and you perhaps do not understand our ways. But believe me when I tell you, you could be executed for making such a remark. Chicahua is not a boy but the living embodiment of the gods, and you would do well to watch your tongue.'

Nelson muttered something under his breath, but then lifted his head and nodded sullenly. Alec could see that his cheek was bright red where the old man's hand had connected with it. Travers straightened up and turned towards the emperor to find Itztli bowing low to him. The high priest spoke in a loud, aggressive tone and kept pointing accusingly towards the captives.

'Looks like Laughing Boy is talking about us,' murmured Ethan.

'Yes, and he doesn't appear to be praising us for our excellent manners,' said Coates.

'Most likely he's asking for permission to sacrifice us,' said Alec glumly.

Ethan looked at him in alarm. 'You think so?' he asked.

Alec nodded. Itztli had pulled out a black stone dagger, which he now held up above his head so that the crowd below could see it. At once there was a great roar of approval.

'Sounds like the crowd's on his side,' said Ethan nervously.

Alec was trying desperately to think of a way out of this mess. Suddenly he had an idea – a desperate measure for sure, but their situation *was* desperate. He slipped a hand into his pocket and found what he was looking for: the round, smooth shape of his compass.

'I'm going to try something,' he told Ethan.

And with that, he stood up and began to climb the steps towards the emperor.

Chapter Fifteen

The Emperor Speaks

There was a moment when everything seemed completely frozen, like a tableau in a waxwork museum: Ethan and Coates stared at Alec in horrified dismay, their mouths open to shout a warning; Travers had half turned to glare at him; Itztli was holding the obsidian dagger above his head and his mouth was open, framing a warning; Tlaloc was crouching down, his brutish face registering amazement.

But Alec continued to climb, one hand outstretched in front of him, the compass glittering in his open palm. He was forcing a smile onto his face – though he feared it looked more like a grimace.

Then the guards blurred into motion. Those standing beside him lifted their spears. Those on the raised platform ran forward to defend their emperor, and Alec found himself looking up at a half-circle of glittering obsidian spear-heads, all pointed at his chest. But he kept moving forward, telling himself that if he hesitated for one moment, all would be lost.

Behind him, Ethan and Coates tried to get to their feet, but they were immediately forced down again. Alec reached the platform and continued to walk towards Chicahua. Itztli shouted an order and the guards in front of Alec raised their spears, ready to throw. Alec just had time to reflect that maybe his idea hadn't been such a good one when a child's voice rang out in the silence — just one word of Nahuatl that Alec didn't understand, but its meaning instantly became clear: the guards lowered their weapons and reluctantly moved back.

At first Alec thought it was the emperor who had spoken, but now he realized that it was the young girl. She bent over to whisper something in Chicahua's ear and the boy nodded. He leaned forward on his throne and smiled at Alec, beckoning him forward with a plump, bejewelled hand. Alec was uncomfortably aware that the bald man with the jaguar on a rope was standing beside the throne, looking at him with an expression of distaste on his face; the jaguar didn't look particularly friendly either.

'Come closer,' said Chicahua.

Alec hesitated for a moment, surprised to find yet another English speaker in this place. He glanced at Travers, who smiled and inclined his head.

'My two keenest students,' he said.

Alec approached the throne and placed the heavy brass compass in Chicahua's hand. As he did so, he experienced a faint twinge of regret. He had loved that compass; but if it got him and his friends out of their current fix, it would be a small price to pay. And he could always get another one.

Chicahua studied the compass thoughtfully, watching as the silver needle twitched and shuddered towards magnetic north. 'What is it?' he asked, intrigued.

'It's a compass,' Alec told him. He was uncomfortably aware that the young girl was studying him with her dark brown eyes, a smile on her face. She was strikingly pretty, her long black hair hanging in braids around her shoulders.

'A cum-pass?' echoed Chicahua, looking puzzled.

'It's a device for . . . finding your way when you are lost. You see how the needle always points to the north?'

'Norf?' Chicahua looked baffled. 'What is this . . . norf?'

Alec shook his head, wondering how he could explain such a thing to an Aztec. He gave it his best shot: 'Wherever you travel,' he said, 'this needle will always show you the best path to take.'

Chicahua studied the compass for a moment and then lifted his head and smiled. 'I see . . .' He nodded. 'That is a fine gift.'

Itztli didn't seem to think so. He stepped forward, pointed at the compass and said something in Nahuatl; it didn't sound complimentary.

'The priest says that this thing is cursed,' said the girl quietly. 'He tells us that we should throw it away.'

'Don't listen to him,' Alec urged her. 'This was given to me by my own father. Don't trust what the priest says.'

She studied Alec for a moment and then nodded. 'I have told my brother this many times,' she said. 'Itztli is a man who smiles with his teeth, but not with his eyes. My brother trusts him, but in my heart I think he wishes us harm.'

'No, sister!' protested Chicahua. 'Itztli is my friend and protector. He gives me wonderful gifts. He sent me a new wife yesterday.'

The girl rolled her eyes as though she could hardly believe what her brother had just said. 'He flatters you because he knows how easily impressed you are.'

Of the two children, she was by far the more accomplished English-speaker, Alec noticed. Her brother sounded crude and halting beside her, but then she must be a good three years older than him.

Itztli came closer now and started to speak rapidly in Nahuatl, pointing at Alec with his dagger as he did so. His face was contorted in an expression of disgust, as though he were discussing the fate of an insect.

Chicahua glanced warily at Alec. 'Itztli asks to kill you and your friends,' he said.

'I understand,' said Alec, looking gravely at the boy. 'Please don't let him.'

Chicahua frowned. 'Itztli is powerful man in Colotlán,' he said doubtfully. 'Is not wise to make of him an enemy.'

'But you are emperor,' said the girl. 'Why not show him who is in charge?'

'Tepin, I tell you before,' said Chicahua. 'You are just a girl. Is not your place to speak of such matters.'

Tepin looked indignant at this. 'I am your sister and I want only the best for you. You should listen to me more often.' She looked at Alec thoughtfully. 'You are handsome,' she said. 'I like your pale skin. What is your name?'

Alec felt his face reddening, but sensing that he had a potential ally in her, he told her, 'My name is Alec.'

'Al-eck,' she said. 'I like your name! What does it mean?'

'Erm . . . I'm not sure,' he said. He thought for a moment. 'I think it means . . . trustworthy. Yes, a man who can be trusted.' He was sure it didn't mean anything of the kind, but he was trying to win them over, so it seemed like the right thing to say.

'My name is Tepin, which means "little one".'

Alec looked at her. 'That's a nice name,' he said

and saw her smile deepen. 'Can't you persuade the priest to spare us?' he begged her.

Tepin leaned over and whispered more words into her brother's ear. Chicahua nodded and turned to Alec.

'Tepin reminds me that we both wish to know more of your world,' he said. 'Coyotl does not speak of his days among the white people. We have asked him many times but he tells us only a little.'

Alec was momentarily puzzled, but then remembered that Coyotl was Travers' Aztec name. 'My world has changed much since his time,' he said. 'I can tell you many things about it. Things that will amaze you.'

There was a silence and then the bald man said something to the emperor. He spoke in Nahuatl, but from the expression on his face Alec surmised that he was warning the boy not to trust this outsider. Chicahua said something terse back to him and he bowed his head in acceptance, but looked none too pleased.

'Patli warns me not to anger Itztli,' said Chicahua. 'Patli is my . . .' He seemed to search for a suitable word and looked to his sister for help.

'I think you call this a . . . servant?' said Tepin.

Alec nodded. 'A servant tells you what to do?' he asked slyly.

Chicahua looked angry. '*Nobody* tells me what to do,' he said. 'I am emperor. I am all-powerful!' He looked at the bald man again and snapped a few more words of Nahuatl. Patli immediately let go of the jaguar's lead and dropped onto his hands and knees, his head bowed until he was within biting distance of the big cat. To emphasize the point, Chicahua lifted a sandaled foot and placed it on the back of Patli's neck. Alec thought what a miserable life it must be for a grown man, dependent on the whims of a twelve-year-old. Chicahua kept his foot there for a moment, then pushed the man away with a sneer.

He considered for a moment, then glanced at Alec. 'Perhaps I ask Itztli for *your* life,' he said. He gestured down the steps to the kneeling captives. 'And I give him the lives of these others.'

Alec shook his head. 'They are my friends,' he said. 'My place is with them.'

'Even if they go to Mictlan?' asked Tepin incredulously.

Alec took a deep breath, realizing that it

would be so easy to wash his hands of it all and save his own skin. But he knew he wouldn't be able to live with himself if he chose that path.

'We are together,' he said. 'If they must go, then I go with them.'

Tepin stared at Alec as though she couldn't quite believe that anyone would make such a choice. Then she smiled again. She said something in Nahuatl to Chicahua, her voice pleading, and he considered her words for a moment. Then he turned to say something to Itztli. The high priest reacted as though he had been slapped. He took a step back and glared at his emperor. When he spoke, his tone was agitated. He pointed to the summit of the step pyramid and lifted the dagger again. Another cheer rose from the crowd, but this time it was more subdued, as though the people weren't sure who they should support.

Chicahua raised an arm and the crowd fell silent. There was a brief pause while he sat there looking around, as if daring them to cheer again. Then he turned back to Itztli and spoke, his child's voice sounding suddenly more authoritative.

Itztli flashed Alec a look of pure venom, but

had to bow his head in acceptance. He turned and descended the steps, striding away into the midst of the crowd, which parted to allow him through.

'What did you say to him?' asked Alec.

'I tell him . . . I need time to . . . decide.'

'Time?' Alec licked his lips. 'How much time?'

'Three days and three nights,' said Chicahua. 'Then we see. Now . . . you come with us, tell us all about your world.'

Alec nodded. 'And . . . my friends?'

'Oh, they go back to . . .' Chicahua seemed to have trouble finding the right word. He mimed bars with his hands.

'Prison?' suggested Alec.

Chicahua shrugged and nodded. 'Don' worry,' he said. 'They be looked after. Plenty to eat and drink.'

'May I speak to them first?'

Chicahua looked somewhat irritated by this request. 'Quickly then,' he said.

Alec turned and hurried down the steps to the others. They all looked up at him with bewildered expressions.

'Master Alec,' said Coates, 'if you ever pull a stunt like that again—'

Alec interrupted him. 'There's not much time,' he said. 'I've got us a reprieve. Three days and three nights. It's not much, but it's something. You're going to be taken back to the cell.'

'And you?' asked Ethan.

'I'm going with the emperor and his sister. They want to know all about us. Meanwhile I'll be trying my best to think of a way to get us out of here.'

'Don't take any risks, Alec,' said Ethan. 'Try and stay on their good side. He may be just a kid, but he's the power in this place. Mind you, I think the sister has a soft spot for you. Maybe you could use that.'

'You think so?' murmured Alec. He glanced back and saw that Tepin was still studying him intently. He gave Ethan and Coates what he hoped was a confident smile.

'Whatever made you think of giving him the compass?' asked Coates.

'I just figured it was something that any boy would like to have.'

'Al-eck!' shouted Chicahua. 'We go now!'

Alec turned obediently, realizing that their fate now lay in the chubby hands of a little boy. He climbed the steps and watched as the slaves shouldered the throne, the guards forming protective rows on either side of their emperor.

Tepin beckoned to Alec. 'You may walk beside me,' she said. Alec bowed respectfully and drew alongside her. As the procession moved off, he risked a quick glance over his shoulder: the guards were marching the others back through the crowd towards their cell. He hoped they'd be all right.

'Don't worry,' said Tepin, noticing his look of concern. 'They will be well looked after. Nothing happens to them without my brother's word.' She studied him again for a moment. 'I like your hair,' she added.

Alec didn't really know what to say to that.

Conchita was annoyed. No sooner had she got back to her chambers to tuck into some hot food (taking care to avoid anything she couldn't easily identify) than her fellow wives were flocking around, urging her to get herself ready for yet another 'special' occasion.

She was feeling bad after witnessing the plight of Frank and the other hostages out in the square. They had all looked terrified and it was clear that their lives were in danger; it made her realize how lucky she was: *her* only problem was deciding which dress to wear. Of course, she still wanted to escape, the first chance she got, but at least she was being well looked after. All right, she had accidentally eaten some dog, but that seemed a small thing compared to the woes of her fellow travellers. At one point Frank had spotted her in the crowd and waved at her and her heart had gone out to him. She had even tried to make her way towards him, but the other wives had grabbed her arms to stop her. Nelli told her that it was forbidden for her to leave the company of her fellow wives except by direct invitation of the emperor. Why, she wondered, was it only now that she realized how special Frank was and how much he meant to her?

Then she had asked, quite innocently, 'Where *is* the emperor, anyhow? All I can see up there is a fat little kid sitting on a golden chair!' The remark had prompted a gasp of horror from Nelli, who had told her quietly and firmly that the 'fat kid' was now her husband and she would do well to make sure nobody heard her speaking about him in such an impudent way.

Conchita had stood there, staring up at the boy, telling herself that at least the fears she'd had about being pushed around by her new husband wouldn't come to much. He looked like he needed help to tie his sandals. She had never thought about getting married, but figured that Rudolph Valentino was nearer to her ideal man. Of course, she knew how Frank felt about her, though neither of them had ever spoken about it. The truth was, she saw Frank as a means to an end – someone with the connections to get her that all-important screen test. But seeing him down on his knees in the square had made her feel terrible, particularly when she saw that he was more concerned about her than he was for himself. She was relieved when she saw the captives being led away – it appeared nothing was happening to them immediately.

Conchita had gone back to her quarters, her empty stomach reminding her that she had gone out without breakfast this morning; and now, here she was, about to bite into her first corn pancake of the day, and Nelli was telling her to get herself dressed at once, because her husband had asked to see his new bride and it didn't do to keep him waiting.

'Give me a break!' complained Conchita. 'Always everything has to be done in the big hurry! Can't I just sit here and finish my breakfas'?'

'No! Now come!' Nelli insisted she change her dress for something more opulent. Then her hair was re-braided – though she was allowed to snack while she sat there being beautified.

'What's going to happen?' she asked Nelli, between bites. 'To Frank and the others?'

Nelli shrugged. 'Chicahua decide in three days. Itztli want to send them to Mictlan.'

'Oh, where's that?' asked Conchita. 'Another town?'

Nelli laughed, showing her perfect white teeth. 'You so funny!' she cried. 'Mictlan is the underworld. Itztli will send them there with his dagger.'

Conchita stared at her. 'But . . . he can't do that!' she protested.

'He can! Itztli has sent many, many people to Mictlan this way.'

Conchita frowned. 'Listen, Nelli. Can you get me in to see Frank?'

Nelli frowned. 'Why you want see him? He not your husban' no more. You have new husban' now.'

Conchita leaned forward in her chair and

placed an arm on Nelli's shoulder. 'You could get me in to talk to him, couldn't you? Just to let him know I'm all right?'

Nelli looked very doubtful. 'We will see,' she said dismissively. 'Right now you must go visit with the emperor. Now, stand up, show me.'

Conchita got to her feet and did a couple of twirls for Nelli, who clapped her hands delightedly. 'Good,' she said. 'Now. We go!'

And before Conchita could say any more, she was being hurried along to a different part of the palace, munching a last corn pancake as she went.

CHAPTER SIXTEEN

Playing for Time

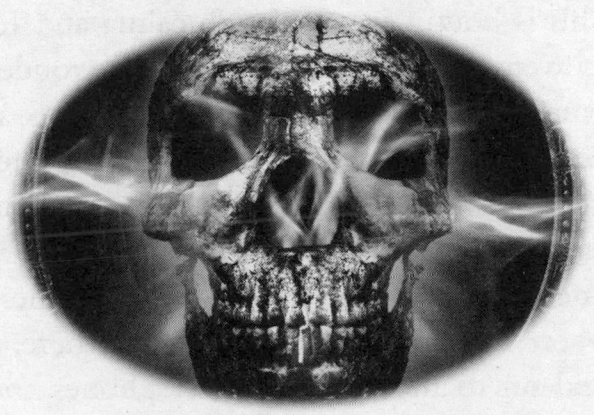

Alec was beginning to feel a bit like Scheherazade, the storyteller from *The Thousand and One Nights*. It had been his favourite bedtime book when he was little, read to him every evening by his mother.

The incredible tales of thieves and magicians and monsters were told by Scheherazade, who had been given in marriage to the king of Persia, only to discover that he'd been taking a new wife every day, then having her head chopped off at dawn so he could be free to marry again. However, Scheherazade told such incredible stories that he could not wait to hear the next one; and for one thousand and one nights she managed to keep him spellbound, until eventually he decided not to kill her.

This is how it was with Chicahua and Tepin. They were eager to hear all about the wonders of the modern world. Alec had begun with aeroplanes – or 'flying chariots' as Chicahua preferred to call them – though describing the workings of an engine to a couple of young Aztecs had taxed his descriptive powers; any bits that he was hazy on he simply made up. From there, they moved on to motorcars and telephones and all manner of inventions that must have sounded like witchcraft to them.

Alec and Chicahua were stretched out on luxurious couches in the emperor's chamber. Tepin stood by her brother's couch, apparently prohibited from taking a seat – though it was becoming clear that she exerted a big influence over her brother; and by the way she kept smiling at Alec, it was obvious that she was more than a little interested in him.

Alec couldn't help feeling guilty when he thought of his friends, cooped up in rather less comfortable circumstances. Chicahua was being waited on by the ever-attentive Patli; the servant kept scowling at Alec, who was worried he might take the opportunity to put poison in his food. Two armed guards stood just a short distance away, their faces impassive – though they were watching Alec intently. At least the jaguar had been put in a cage, where he was gnawing on a large chunk of meat. Alec had been told that he was called Yaotl and was Chicahua's pet, raised from a cub to be his protector.

On a low table beside the emperor were all manner of exotic snacks, most of which Alec could not identify; a couple of golden goblets were filled with something called *pulque*, a rather bitter-tasting beer which, if Alec understood correctly, was made from cactus. He wasn't at all sure that a twelve-year-old should be drinking such a powerful brew. The couple of polite sips he had taken had made him feel distinctly light-headed. Chicahua also had a thing about chocolate. A huge bowl of cocoa beans stood in front of him, and every so often he would gesture to Patli, who would obediently place one in the boy's mouth. This might account for Chicahua's weight problem, Alec thought. He was pudgier than the average twelve-year-old had any right to be. When prompted, Alec helped himself to a couple of the beans but they were so bitter he felt like gagging and eventually had to pretend to eat them, while surreptitiously putting them in his pocket.

Chicahua and Tepin weren't content to just listen. Alec's stories were punctuated by a whole string of awkward questions.

'So what makes these car things go?' asked Chicahua at one point.

'Well, they have an engine. A thing made of metal with many moving parts. And when you put petrol into it—'

'Pet-rol. What is pet-rol?' asked Tepin.

'It's a liquid made from oil.'

'Oil?'

'Umm . . . yes, crude oil. That's a black sticky substance that comes from deep underground. People have to dig down far below the surface to find it. Anyway, they take this crude oil and they refine it—'

'Refine it?' muttered Chicahua.

'They . . . er . . . clean it up. Take all the stickiness out of it. And once they've done that, it's called petrol and they pour it into a tank in the car and it's fed into the engine. The liquid gives off a gas. Then a spark ignites the gas—'

'Ignites it?' asked Tepin.

'Yes, it sort of . . . . sets fire to it. In a controlled way. And that drives a piston up and down—'

'Piston?'

And so on. Alec could very easily have lost his temper with them, but he knew that would be a big mistake so he went on answering their questions with good grace. He was quite relieved when they were interrupted by a young woman, who came in, head bowed low. She said something to Patli. He in turn passed on the message and Chicahua nodded.

'Wait,' he told Alec. 'I have to meet new wife.'

Alec stared at the boy, amazed to think that anyone that age might have even *one* wife, let alone several. And then he remembered who that new wife was. He turned to look as Conchita was led into the room by a couple of other women. She stood there, looking from Chicahua to Alec and back again. She'd been dressed in an exquisitely embroidered robe, her hair braided and her cheeks rouged. She did look very attractive, Alec thought – apart from the scowl on her face, as if she had just detected a bad smell in the room. Clearly the thought of being married to a twelve-year-old boy didn't exactly thrill her.

Alec hoped she wouldn't say anything out of turn, but then he remembered what she was like. This situation called for diplomacy, something she didn't exactly have an abundance of.

Chicahua studied her thoughtfully. 'You are pretty,' he said at last.

Conchita didn't reply. She just glared back at him as if he'd said she was the ugliest creature he'd ever set eyes on.

'But she looks cross,' added Tepin warily. 'You don't want another cross wife, brother. Remember that other one you had?'

Chicahua nodded. He looked at Alec. 'I had to get rid of her,' he said.

Alec winced. He could only imagine what that meant, but he was pretty sure she hadn't been sent off to a nice hotel.

Conchita looked at Alec. 'What are you doing here?' she asked him.

'I . . . er . . . I'm telling the great emperor and his sister all about life in our world,' he said.

'Yeah?' muttered Conchita. 'Well, maybe you could find out when they're going to let us get back to it.'

Chicahua laughed. 'But you are going nowhere,' he said. 'You my wife now, your place here.'

Conchita shook her head. 'I'm not being funny, Chicasaw, or whatever your name is, but when it comes to men, I look for somebody a little more mature — you know what I mean?'

Alec nearly buried his face in his hands.

'You funny,' Chicahua said. 'I think we will get on well.'

Tepin didn't seem quite as impressed. 'She does not seem to respect you, brother,' she said. 'Perhaps you should have her beaten.'

'Beaten?' gasped Conchita; her eyes seemed to be daring the young emperor to even try such a thing.

Chicahua waved a hand in dismissal. 'It is no matter. She will need to get used to our ways.' He looked at Conchita. 'Now you will dance for me.'

Her jaw dropped in astonishment. 'Dance?' she cried.

'All his wives dance for him,' said Tepin. 'It is Aztec way. You will do this or you will be beaten.' She clapped her hands and shouted something in Nahuatl.

Alec could see that Conchita was about to hit the roof, so he quickly got up. 'Great Emperor,' he said, 'your new wife is . . . unfamiliar with the

Aztec ways. If I might be allowed to have a quick word with her?'

Chicahua shrugged his plump shoulders and Alec hurried across to Conchita. He grabbed her by the wrist and pulled her over to the other side of the room.

'Hey, whaddya doing?' she protested, but Alec ignored her.

'Listen,' he said quietly. 'You have to do this. It may be humiliating, but that boy over there has the power to have us all killed just by clicking his fingers.'

Conchita glared back at him. 'But I will feel stupid,' she said.

'Better that than being dead. What do you suppose happened to that cross wife he was talking about?'

Conchita's eyes widened in realization. 'Oh,' she said.

A small group of musicians was trooping into the room, carrying a selection of exotic-looking instruments. Conchita looked at them blankly. 'But I don't know how to—'

'Conchita, just imagine that the emperor is whatsisname. Louis B. Mayer. Think of this as your screen test!'

'But—'

'You know how to dance, don't you? Didn't Frank say he first saw you in a musical revue?'

'Sure, but . . .' She looked at the musicians, who were now settling themselves down on the floor. 'Do they look like they know the music of Irving Berlin?' she asked him.

'No, but you'll just have to improvise.' He gazed at her intently. 'Please, Conchita, I'm begging you. All our lives might depend on this dance.'

'Oh, so no pressure then,' she said flatly.

Alec went back to his couch, hoping against hope that he'd managed to get through to her. Conchita turned back to face the emperor.

He clapped his hands once and the musicians started to play a weird composition, consisting of a lively drum beat with pan pipes and ocarinas. It didn't sound like anything that Alec had ever heard before, and certainly nothing like Irving Berlin.

Conchita closed her eyes for a moment. She seemed to be concentrating, and for a very long time she didn't move so much as a muscle. Alec glanced nervously at Chicahua and saw that he was frowning. But then Conchita began to move, swinging her arms, undulating this way and that across the floor. They were the kind of steps you might expect to see in any modern musical revue, but set against the wild cacophony that accompanied her they looked positively surreal. However, Conchita seemed to grow in confidence, adapting the moves to suit the unfamiliar beat. Just when it seemed it couldn't get any more bizarre, she began to sing.

> 'Welcome to Acapulco
> Your playground in the sun.
> Come and join us, on the beaches
> And we'll have a lot of fun!
> We'll go swimming in the ocean
> We'll go dancing every night
> To the sounds of Latin Salsa
> Everything will be all right.
> Acapulco! Acapulco!
> Your playground in the sun!
> Come and join us, come and join us
> And we'll have a lot of fun!'

Chicahua looked at the baffled expression on Alec's face; he could only smile back desperately. 'A traditional song from our world, your highness,' he shouted, over the fearsome racket of the musicians. 'Especially in your honour.'

'Ah!' Chicahua nodded and seemed perfectly happy. He and Tepin began to clap along to the music, while Conchita whirled backwards and forwards, singing her heart out. It struck Alec that though he had experienced some strange events in Egypt, nothing that had happened to him there quite compared to this.

Back in their cell, Ethan, Coates and the others were unable to settle. The sky they could see through the grille above them had darkened and the first stars were out. Most of them were sitting on their bunks, but sleep seemed a million miles away. Coates was worried about Alec, and Frank was equally concerned about Conchita. But whereas the valet was able to keep his troubles to himself, Frank was more vocal. He strode up and down the room, complaining to anybody who would listen.

'It ain't right,' he kept saying. 'You can't just take somebody against their will and marry them off to some little kid.'

'They can do whatever they want,' Ethan told him. 'They're the ones with the knives and spears.'

'But that don't make it *right*. She must be terrified. God only knows what those savages are putting her through.'

'Will you shut up?' growled Nelson ungraciously. 'That woman is most likely living in the lap of luxury now. She's got it easy. She isn't the one with a death sentence hanging over her.'

Frank glared at him. 'Oh, that's you all over, isn't it?' he said. 'Don't care nothin' about nobody 'cept yourself.'

'Yeah, I look out for number one,' admitted Nelson. 'Always have, always will. That's how I got where I am today.'

'Stuck in a cell,' observed Coates. 'Nice work, Mr Nelson. You'll excuse me if I don't applaud. And let's not forget that Master Alec is out there too. And if it hadn't been for him, we'd probably all be history by now.'

Nelson shrugged. 'The kid's plucky, I'll give him that. Reminds me of myself at that age.'

Luis gave him a look of disbelief. 'You are kidding, I hope. That boy's got more to him than you'll ever have. I figure you've always been what you are now. A user.'

Nelson studied Luis contemptuously. 'Oh, so you've finally plucked up the courage to say something, have you? I thought maybe you'd realized that nobody here gives a tinker's cuss what you think.'

'I tell you what I think,' said Luis calmly. 'I think there's a way out of here and we should be spending our time trying to find it.'

'Amen to that,' said Ethan. 'Here's how I figure it. Supposing a couple of us pretend to have a fight? The guards rush in here to break it up, we overpower them and make a run for it.'

'And go where, exactly?' asked Coates. 'We're in a city in the middle of a jungle — there'd be nowhere to run to.'

Ethan turned to look at him. 'On the way here we passed a river,' he said. 'There were canoes moored by a jetty. We'd grab ourselves a couple of those and take off downstream. Of course, we'd have to locate Alec and Conchita first — there's no way we'd leave them behind. But all rivers lead eventually to the sea, and there'll be villages near the coast. Friendly ones. We'd just have to make it to one of them.'

Nelson stretched out his arms. 'Oh, so easy!' he exclaimed. 'Yeah, just the small matter of paddling a boat several hundred miles. Should be a piece of cake!'

Ethan sighed. 'You got a better idea, I'd love to hear it.'

'Yeah, I got one,' said Nelson. 'These people speak English, don't they?'

'Some of 'em do,' agreed Frank.

'So then, they can be bargained with. Every civilization, no matter how primitive, understands the principles of business. Back in Veracruz I have millions of dollars at my disposal. Millions! We just get them to name their price to let us go. I can arrange to have the money brought here and—'

Luis laughed in disbelief. 'You think these people care about your stinking money?' he cried. 'They are planning to send us to their god, Señor Nelson. It may surprise you to know that their religion has nothing to do with commerce. And besides, what good would money do them, way out here? There's no shops for them to spend it in. No Macy's, no Sears, no ice-cold Coca-Cola!'

'It doesn't have to be money!' protested Nelson. 'Gold! Bars of gold. Everybody understands gold. Or we could offer them trinkets – bracelets, necklaces; anything they want, I can get it for them!'

Luis shook his head. 'I don't know who is more pathetic. You for saying such stupid things or us for even listening to you!'

The colour seemed to drain out of Nelson's face. Suddenly he leaped off his bunk and flung himself at the Mexican, slamming him against the wall. Luis struggled to escape but Nelson's hands were clamped tight around his throat, trying to throttle the life out of him. There was a moment's hesitation from everyone else and then a mad scramble to try and pull the two men apart. It took some time to disentangle them. In the midst of it all, Ethan looked hopefully towards the door, expecting a guard to rush in to see what all the commotion was, but nobody did. It seemed as if their captors were quite happy to let them fight amongst themselves.

'So much for that theory,' he muttered. He flung Nelson onto his own bunk, while Coates and Frank settled Luis back onto his. 'Nice of you boys to try and cause a diversion,' he said sarcastically.

The two men sat glowering at each other in mutual hatred.

'If we ever get out of this, I'm going to fix you good,' said Nelson.

'You are welcome to try,' said Luis quietly.

In the following silence the sound of the door opening made everybody sit up and take notice. Alec stepped into the room and the door was slammed and bolted behind him.

'Master Alec,' said Coates. 'Thank goodness you're all right. Did anybody try to harm you?'

'No, I'm fine,' Alec assured him. 'Really. I've been spending time with Chicahua and his sister. Luckily they seem to like me.'

'Oh, they like you,' said Nelson. 'We're all thrilled to hear that.'

Ethan shot him a look. 'Button it,' he said. 'Or you and me are gonna be slugging it out.'

'Did you see anything of Conchita?' asked Frank anxiously.

'Er . . . yes, don't worry, she's doing fine.'

'Where exactly did you see her?' persisted Frank.

'In the emperor's palace. She was . . . er . . . singing and dancing.'

'She was *what*?' asked Ethan incredulously.

'She was doing excerpts from *Welcome to Acapulco*,' said Alec. 'It was, er . . . well, you had to be there.'

'You see,' said Nelson bitterly. 'I knew that one

would land on her feet. We're stuck here on death row and she's living the life of Riley. I guess we can forget about getting any help from her.'

Frank looked at him. 'I'm just goin' to ignore that,' he said.

'Too right,' said Ethan, looking sternly around at his companions. 'The way I figure it, we've already lost one day, and if we carry on fighting and bickering amongst ourselves, we'll have no chance of getting out of here.'

'So what is your plan?' asked Luis.

'I already told you my plan,' said Ethan. 'OK, it's not great, but the way I see it, we've got two more days to figure out a better one.'

Everybody considered this in silence for a moment.

Ethan gave Alec a grim look. 'Don't worry, kid,' he said. 'We'll think of something.'

Everyone moved back to their bunks and sat down.

'We don't know for sure we've only got two more days,' said Alec hopefully. 'I think Chicahua likes me. Maybe I could persuade him to spare us.'

Coates frowned. 'It's certainly an idea, Master Alec. But from what I've seen, that high priest is the real power behind the throne. And he seems determined to get his hands on us one way or another. I'm not sure how long a young boy like Chicahua can stand up to somebody like Itztli. I fear he was just putting off the inevitable.'

Alec frowned. He lay down on his bunk and thought about trying to get some sleep. But sleep seemed a million miles away.

CHAPTER SEVENTEEN

The Big Match

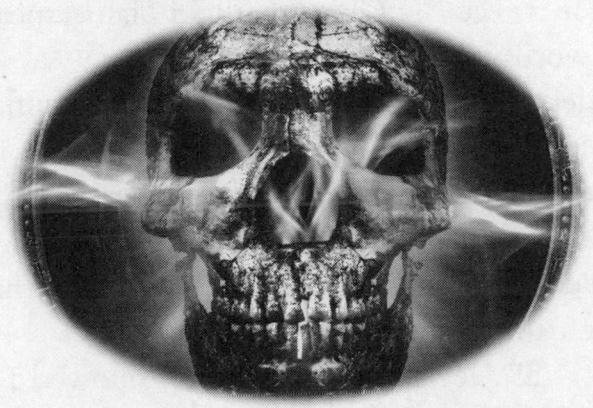

Alec woke to the sound of the cell door opening. Early morning sunlight was pouring in through the bars above him. Sitting up, he saw that several armed guards, led by Tlaloc, had entered the room. For a moment he felt totally disorientated. The last thing he remembered was being unable to sleep, so exactly how and when had he drifted off? Panic flared in the pit of his stomach as he looked at the stern faces of the Aztecs. He wondered if Chicahua's decision had been overturned and they faced death earlier than the appointed time; but Tlaloc simply beckoned to Alec. He got obediently to his feet.

'Where are you taking him?' demanded Coates, starting to get up, but one of the warriors held a spear to his chest, forcing him back.

'He . . . go . . . Chicahua,' said Tlaloc, speaking the words with great care.

Alec felt a sense of relief wash over him. The boy emperor was no doubt eager to hear more about the wonders of the modern world. He smiled reassuringly at the others.

'Put in a good word for us, kid,' said Ethan as he left the room.

'I will!' Alec shouted back. He followed Tlaloc along the whitewashed corridor, noting that there were only a couple of guards minding the cell door, and then they emerged in the main plaza. He looked apprehensively at the step pyramid but it seemed reassuringly deserted today. They crossed the plaza, heading for the royal palace. Two heavily armed jaguar warriors stood on either side of the entrance, but they simply nodded to Tlaloc and allowed them through. Finally they came to the room where Conchita had entertained them the day before, and found Chicahua, Tepin and Travers eating what looked like an enormous breakfast. The three of them were being waited on by some of

Chicahua's wives, but Conchita was not among them. As usual, two more guards stood near the table, keeping an eye on their emperor. Tlaloc bowed to Chicahua and then left the room.

The boy looked up and grinned delightedly, his chin sticky with grease. 'Good morning, Al-eck!' he said. 'Come, you must be hungry, eat with us.'

Alec approached the table, realizing as he did so that he was starving. He had to admit that some of the many platters did look enticing. He took a seat opposite Travers and surveyed the food with interest.

'Help yourself,' said Tepin. 'Just use your fingers.'

Alec selected a corn pancake filled with red beans and began to bite into it hungrily.

'Did you sleep well?' Travers asked him.

Alec gave him a cool look. 'As well as might be expected for somebody who has only a short time to live,' he said bitterly.

Travers shook his head. 'You should not think of it as an end,' he said, 'but a beginning. It is a great honour to be sent to the realm of Mictlan.'

Alec swallowed his mouthful. 'You'll forgive

me if I don't get too excited about it,' he said. He looked at Chicahua. 'You know, your majesty, I have so much more to tell you about the world beyond Colotlán. I . . . I'm not sure that I will have time to tell you everything.'

Chicahua looked thoughtful. 'Well, you must tell me what you can in the time you have,' he said.

This was not the answer Alec had been hoping for. 'But surely there's some way we could . . . extend the deadline?'

Chicahua looked puzzled. 'I do not understand,' he said.

'I think he is asking for more time,' said Tepin.

'Yes. I mean, couldn't we put off the sacrifice for a few more days?'

Chicahua looked at Travers but the old man shook his head.

'You don't know what you are asking,' he said. 'Chicahua has already angered Itztli by making him wait three days.'

'But . . . just exactly who is emperor here?' demanded Alec. 'When all is said and done, Itztli is just a . . . a priest!'

Travers smiled. 'To say such a thing proves that you do not understand the Aztec way of life. In our world, priests are all-powerful. They speak with the gods; they are our guides to their ways. It does not do to anger a priest, especially one as powerful as Itztli. Any Aztec would tell you the same.'

Alec snorted. 'But you're not an Aztec.'

Travers looked irritated by the remark. 'Of course I am,' he snapped.

'No. You're just a . . . a tourist. Pretending to be like these people. I notice *you* managed to evade the knife.'

'Ah, but I would have accepted it gladly if that had been the decision.'

'Oh yes, I'm sure!'

Travers sighed. He looked at Alec sadly. 'I understand it must seem cruel and unjust to one such as yourself. It is not the way of your people. But you wandered into this place—'

'Hardly! We were captured and brought here against our will. That's not the same thing at all.'

Travers made a dismissive gesture. 'I am not going to argue with you,' he said. 'I have advised Chicahua not to put off Itztli any longer.' He glanced sternly at Chicahua. 'I hope that he will take my advice. Now it is for you to spend what time you have wisely.' He made an effort to calm down. 'Actually, we have a little surprise for you. Something we think you may enjoy.' He got up from the table. 'In fact, I must go and prepare myself. I will leave Chicahua to tell you about it,' he finished, and left the room.

Alec sighed. He helped himself to some meat and chewed on it thoughtfully.

'You seem . . . unhappy,' observed Chicahua, and Alec felt like slapping him. How did he expect him to feel? He'd just been told he only had another two days to live. Did the boy expect him to sing and dance? He had to restrain himself from making a sarcastic reply; instead he adopted a pleading tone.

'It's just that I . . . was so looking forward to telling you all about my world,' he said. 'Some of the things I could have shared with you . . . Well, I suppose now you'll never know about them.' He looked hopefully at Tepin, who seemed more sympathetic than her brother. 'I'm sure *you'd* like to hear more of my stories, wouldn't you?'

Tepin smiled back at him. 'I would,' she admitted. 'Very much.' She looked at her brother. 'And I am always telling Chicahua that Itztli has too much power in this city. If you ask me, I think he would like to rule Colotlán in my brother's place.'

Chicahua looked shocked. 'Tepin, you must not say such things!' He glanced nervously at the two guards standing just a short distance away. 'Supposing your words found their way to Itztli's ears?'

Tepin shrugged. 'What if they did? I am not afraid of him, as you are.'

Chicahua looked angry at this. 'Who says I am afraid?' he growled. He picked up a whole corn pancake and stuffed it into his mouth, then spoke through a mouthful of food. 'He must serve his emperor, like all the others.'

'If that's the case, why is he always pushing you around?' asked Alec.

'He is not!' Chicahua seemed about to lose his temper – his sudden outburst caused him to spray bits of half-eaten food across the table. 'Al-eck, if you keep speaking to me in this way, we are going to fall out! Have I not been good to you? Have I not given you three extra days?' He paused for a moment, chewing furiously as he glared across the table at Alec. Then he seemed to relax a little. 'Anyway,' he went on, 'all this shouting will spoil our . . . how do you call it?

Our surprise for you.' He leaned forward with all the eagerness of a twelve-year-old. 'Tell me, Alec . . . do you like sports?'

Alec and Tepin walked along beside Chicahua's gilded throne as eight servants carried it through the crowded streets. On the other side, Patli trotted along with the jaguar on its lead; flanking them were two rows of guards, ready to defend the young emperor with their lives. Anybody who was slow to get out of the way was pushed unceremoniously aside. As the procession moved along, the people bowed their heads respectfully. Some even fell to their knees.

Alec felt an overpowering sense of despair. His time was ticking away and Chicahua had thought it might cheer him up to see the Aztec equivalent of a football match! He had read about the sport, of course – a game called *tlachtli*, but had never expected to actually see it played. Ordinarily he would have been fascinated, but it was going to take something more than this to distract him from the fate that awaited him and his friends. He took the opportunity to work on Tepin a little more.

'You know, it's very sad that I won't be around for much longer,' he said. 'There is so much here that I would love to learn.'

Tepin smiled at him. 'Is there somebody special waiting for you in your world?' she asked him.

'Only my father,' he replied. 'My mother died over a year ago.'

Tepin shook her head. 'No, I meant . . . a . . . what word does Coyotl use? Ah yes, a sweetheart.'

Alec glanced at her nervously, feeling his face reddening. 'Oh no, nothing like that!' he said hastily. 'What, er . . . what about you?'

'It will soon be time for me to marry,' she told him.

Alec knew from his studies that Aztec girls generally married at the age of fifteen, but it was still a shock to hear it said so matter-of-factly. 'Do you, er . . . know who it's going to be?'

She gave him a sad little smile. 'My brother will choose somebody for me,' she said. 'Knowing him, it will probably be one of the jaguar warriors. He admires them.'

Alec glanced doubtfully up at the boy riding on his golden throne. 'Do you think . . . I mean, is that the right way to do it? Wouldn't a warrior be much older than you?'

She nodded. 'It would not be my choice,' she said. 'I would prefer somebody my own age.' And with that she gave Alec such a searching look that he quickly changed the subject.

The procession came to a stone entrance and the servants lowered the throne to the ground so that Chicahua could get down. He led Alec and Tepin up a short flight of steps to a gallery overlooking a large earthen pitch shaped like a huge letter 'I', flanked on the two long sides by high stone walls. As they stepped out, conch shells sounded a raucous fanfare and there was a great roar of approval from the people seated on either side of the pitch. Chicahua waved to the spectators and then took a seat on an opulent throne. Several other chairs were positioned beside it – he gestured to Alec to take the seat to his left, Patli the one to his right, the jaguar curled like an overgrown house cat at his feet. Tepin sat beside Alec. A few moments later Travers arrived, resplendent in colourful robes, and took his place next to Patli. Alec noticed that one chair remained empty; it was almost as grand as the emperor's throne and set a little apart from the others. Sure enough, a few moments later, Itztli stalked into the gallery, and after acknowledging the cheers of the crowd, he took a seat, throwing a contemptuous look at Alec as he did so.

Now servant girls came into the gallery, offering earthenware cups of *pulque* and jugs of sweet chocolate drink. Others bore trays of locusts, sweet cakes and peanuts.

'You have games in your world?' Chicahua asked Alec.

Alec nodded. He told Chicahua a little about the basics of football, rugby and cricket, but he kept the details sketchy, begrudging him too much detail now that he had declined to offer any more help.

'*Tlachtli* is the best sport,' said Chicahua. 'The most skilful game of all. I would love to play myself but they will not let me.'

Alec looked at the boy irritably. 'Who wouldn't let you?' he asked.

'My people. The players get terrible . . . injures?'

'Injuries,' Alec corrected him.

'Yes. And what would happen if I broke my bones? My people would weep. My people love me. Watch this.' He stood up for a moment and waved his arms to the crowd. He was instantly rewarded with great cheers of approval.

'Stop showing off, brother,' said Tepin quietly, and Chicahua sat down again, looking a little deflated.

He looked at Alec curiously. 'The games you spoke of . . . you have played them?'

'Of course,' said Alec. 'At school. Everybody does.'

'Ah.' Chicahua nodded and sighed. 'You are lucky, Al-eck. I cannot do such things. I would love to play *tlachtli*, but I cannot. It is too bad.'

Alec looked at the boy, thinking that for all his power here in Colotlán, he was to be pitied. Overfed and overweight, carried everywhere he wanted to go, he could hardly expect to live a long and healthy life. A regular game of football would probably do him the world of good.

Suddenly a great roar went up below him and Alec saw that the two teams were running onto the pitch – lithe, muscular warriors who wore protective pads on their hips, elbows and around their waists. He counted seven men on each team. They stood waving at the crowd, enjoying the adulation, and then another man appeared holding a rubber ball about the size of a melon. It was evident from the way he carried it that it was very heavy. He spoke briefly to the two teams and then flung the ball high into the air, before turning and running off the pitch.

As the ball descended, the two nearest players leaped into the air to try and reach it, crashing into each other with a force that made Alec wince. They fell back and hit the ground, but a third man caught the ball expertly on his bent knee and hoisted it back into the air; and then there was a free-for-all.

Alec knew that the players were not allowed to touch the ball with their hands — only with their knees, elbows, hips and (rather bizarrely) buttocks; but nothing he had read could have prepared him for the ferocity of the game: it seemed to have no rules and no referee to ensure fair play. He could see that one team wore red cloths around their arms and the other blue, and he knew that the object of the game was to knock the ball through a small upright stone hoop set halfway along the wall on either side of the court.

In mute horror he watched a display of savagery that was more suited to a battlefield than a game. Elbows were smashed into faces, shoulders slammed into chests and ferocious kicks were directed at any part of the body that got in the way of the ball. After a few minutes many players were bleeding and in one particularly fierce tussle a man's leg snapped with a sharp crack that could be heard even over the yells of the spectators. The game was stopped for a moment while the victim was carried off the pitch and another player ran out to take his place, waving to the crowd as he did so. Then the game continued.

'Good, eh?' cried Chicahua, his mouth smeared with cocoa juice, and Alec forced a smile – though in truth he thought it was one of the most horrible spectacles he had ever been obliged to watch. He glanced at Tepin, but she seemed to be enjoying the match as much as her brother, so he threw aside his reservations and tried to enjoy the game for what it was.

And then, despite everything, he started to get caught up in the excitement; and when a player on the red team managed to elbow the ball through one of the stone hoops, he found himself jumping to his feet and cheering along with the others. When he sat down again, he happened to glance at Itztli and felt a chill go through him as he realized that the priest was studying him with a cruel smile on his face. His expression seemed to be saying, *Go on, enjoy yourself while you can, for soon you will be at my mercy.*

Alec felt anger coursing through him and had to fight down the urge to give the high priest a piece of his mind; he realized how pointless that would be. Itztli did not speak English, and even if he asked Travers to translate, there would be nothing Alec could say to change his mind. But there must be *something* he could do, he thought desperately.

An extra loud cheer made him look up: the game was over, and the bruised and bloodied players were waving to the crowd again. Alec had lost track of the score but it was apparent from their gleeful expressions that the red team had won the day. They had left the rubber ball on the pitch, and a sudden crazy idea came to him. Back at school, he'd been pretty good at several ball games. Maybe, just maybe . . .

He glanced slyly at Chicahua. 'They aren't bad players,' he observed, gesturing at the departing teams.

Chicahua looked at him. '*Not bad?*' he cried. 'They are the finest players in Colotlán!'

Alec shrugged. 'In my world we have a game called football,' he said. 'I play it myself. You can only touch the ball with your foot. No elbows, no hips – and definitely none of this . . .' He slapped his backside to emphasize the point and Tepin had to mask a giggle. 'But of course, it takes real skill to play *that* game.' He pointed to one of the stone hoops. 'You see the hoop down there?'

'Yes,' said Chicahua.

'I bet I could get a ball through that hoop three times in a row,' he said.

The emperor followed his gaze. He considered for a moment. 'I don't believe you could,' he said flatly. 'The teams have to practise hard. Ordinary people don't have their skill.'

Alec shrugged. 'It would be easy for me,' he said. 'Child's play.'

Chicahua looked interested and Alec tried to keep his expression blank, not wanting to betray his desperation. There was a long silence.

'And you say you could do it three times . . . one after the other, without missing?' asked Chicahua.

'Yes,' said Alec. 'Easily.'

'All right then.' The boy gestured to the empty court. 'Let me see you do it.'

Alec pretended to be thinking about it. 'Well, I could, of course, but . . . what's in it for me?' he asked at last.

'What do you mean?'

'If I do it, there should be a reward of some kind.'

Chicahua considered for a moment. 'I'll give you cocoa beans,' he said. 'Lots of them.'

Alec shook his head. 'No. I tell you what, if I can do it, you give me and my friends our freedom. What do you say to that?'

Chicahua shook his head. 'Out of the question,' he said. 'The order has been made, I cannot change that.'

Alec frowned. 'All right then. How about three more days before we are sacrificed? That's not too much to ask, is it?'

Chicahua still looked doubtful. 'Itztli would not like it,' he muttered.

'Oh, of course, Itztli!' Alec waved a hand towards the high priest. 'I was forgetting that he's the man who *really* rules Colotlán.'

'That is not true!' protested Chicahua. 'I am emperor. My word is law.'

'In name, perhaps, but . . . you don't seem to have any *real* power.'

'I have so!' the boy snapped indignantly.

Tepin entered the conversation. 'It is very simple, brother,' she said. 'Alec has offered you a bet. You can take it or leave it.'

'That's easy for you to say.' Chicahua glanced towards Itztli, who was watching them suspiciously. 'What if I have to tell Itztli to delay the sacrifice again?'

'Alec is right,' said Tepin. 'It *is* Itztli who commands this city.'

'It is not!' protested her brother. 'I am emperor.' He stood up. 'Very well, Alec − do it three times and you and your friends shall have three more days.'

'You give your word?' asked Alec.

'Of course.' Chicahua laughed. 'You won't do it anyway. Even our best players could not do such a thing.'

Alec wanted to make sure about this. 'You swear to me that if I can get the ball through the hoop three times, you will delay the sacrifice for another three days?'

'Yes!' said Chicahua impatiently. 'I have already said it shall be so.'

'Right then.' Alec got up and, in one swift movement, clambered over the gallery wall and dropped down onto the pitch some six feet below. A wild murmur of excitement went up from the spectators. Many of them had been leaving, but now they hurried back to their seats to see what was going on.

Alec walked over to the ball and picked it up, gauging its weight. As he had suspected, it was much too heavy to kick – it was solid enough to break an ankle. He bounced it a couple of times on the hard-packed ground, but it didn't rise more than a foot or so. Then he turned and judged the height of the hoop. Luckily one of the other games he had played at school was the American sport of basketball.

He took a deep breath, then ran forward quickly. He leaped high in the air and threw the ball straight through the hoop.

A gasp of surprise came from the crowd. Alec trotted after the ball, caught it and walked back to his starting position. As he steadied himself for his next shot, he noticed that Chicahua and Tepin had come to the edge of the gallery and were staring down at him. Chicahua looked outraged.

'You . . . you cheated!' he cried. 'You used your hands.'

Alec gazed up at him, an expression of innocence on his face. 'But your majesty, I never said I wouldn't.'

He ran forward again, leaped up a second time and threw the ball. This time it didn't go through the hoop quite so cleanly. It glanced against the edge first, and Alec ran forward and caught it. He walked back to his starting position, telling himself that he must make absolutely sure of his third shot. So much depended on it.

Chicahua was waiting for him, and this time Travers was standing beside him. 'You spoke of feet-ball!' cried the emperor. 'You said you would *kick* the ball through the hoop.'

Alec shook his head. 'No, your majesty, you are mistaken. I *mentioned* football, but I only said I could get the ball through the hoop three times. I didn't say how.' He lifted the ball. 'Nobody could kick it through – it's far too heavy.'

Tepin had a big grin on her face and Travers was looking down at Alec with the ghost of a smile.

'Perhaps it is you who should be called

Coyotl,' he said, and Alec thought he detected a note of admiration in his voice.

'The emperor promised,' he reminded the old man, and Travers bowed his head.

Alec turned and studied the hoop. Only now, when it actually mattered, did he realize what a small target it was. Sweat trickled down his face and neck. If he missed this shot, he reminded himself, it would all have been for nothing.

Time seemed to stand still and the noise of the crowd faded away. For an instant he was back in the gymnasium at school, preparing to take the shot that would give his team the trophy. Basketball was relatively new in England and his school had been one of the first to take it up. He could smell the varnished wood floor beneath him; above the hoop he saw the big clock announcing that there were only a few more minutes of play left.

Then the world came back into focus. He was in the unfamiliar *tlachtli* arena and the sun was beating down upon his unprotected head. Sweat oozed from every pore, making his khaki shirt stick to his back. He took a breath, ran forward and leaped into the air.

Everything seemed to happen in slow motion.

He saw the heavy rubber ball flying up; as he dropped to the ground, he saw it hit the lip of the ring; he saw it bounce to one side and hit the far edge; saw it settle on the bottom curve of the ring as though it planned to stop there. Then, slowly . . . slowly . . . the ball rolled forward and dropped through the hoop.

A great roar of approval rose from the crowd and Alec lifted his arms in a gesture of triumph. He turned to look towards the royal gallery and saw that Itztli was on his feet, talking angrily to Chicahua and Travers. Tepin was laughing delightedly at Alec's deception. Chicahua looked defiant, Travers troubled, Itztli quite obviously furious. He pointed down at Alec and his voice rose, but Chicahua was shaking his head and shrugging his plump little shoulders, clearly refusing to go back on his word. Itztli directed a look of pure venom in Alec's direction and Alec could not resist the temptation to give him a cheery wave.

Itztli said something else, then turned and strode away. Now Travers and Chicahua were talking earnestly to each other, but the boy kept shaking his head — Alec realized he was insisting that he had given his word and that the bet must be honoured. Tepin came to stand by the gallery and smiled down at Alec.

Alec suddenly heard footsteps behind him and turned to see that Tlaloc had entered the arena. His face was as expressionless as ever, but he beckoned to Alec, who knew better than to disobey.

CHAPTER EIGHTEEN

Repercussions

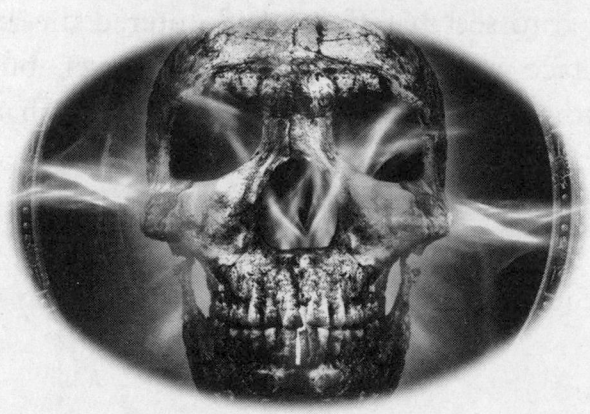

U p in the gallery, the others were waiting for him. Chicahua looked furious. He was pacing up and down, his chubby little face set into a scowl.

'You tricked me!' he said as Alec approached him.

'Your majesty, I think you misunderstood what I was saying,' protested Alec. 'I only said that I—'

'I know what you said! But now Itztli is very angry. I have never seen him so angry. And I had to tell him that I could not go back on my word.'

'Try to see it from my point of view,' said Alec.

'Imagine if it was you being sent to your death. You'd have done the same thing.'

But Chicahua was shaking his head. 'I offered you the hand of friendship,' he snarled. 'And this is how you choose to repay me. Well, that's it! Our friendship is no more. I shall not send for you again. I don't care how many wonders you can describe, I do not wish to hear your voice any more!'

'Brother,' said Tepin, 'you are only angry because Alec got the better of you. You have to admit he *was* very clever.'

'Quiet, Tepin!' snapped Chicahua. 'Keep out of this. It's time you learned your place. It was you who talked me into taking that bet.' He turned back to glare at Alec. 'Now it is over. You shall go back to your friends and the next time you come out of your prison, it will be to meet your death.' He glanced around at the others. 'Come, we go!' he snapped and went quickly towards the exit.

Patli shot a triumphant look at Alec and then scurried after his master, pulling the jaguar behind him. Travers studied Alec for a moment and then gave him a sad smile.

'I hope you enjoy your three extra days,' he said. 'You may choose to spend them reflecting on how devious you have been.' He turned away and followed the emperor.

Only Tepin hung back, looking at Alec solemnly. 'I am sorry it has to end like this,' she said.

Alec shrugged. 'Me too. Perhaps when Chicahua's had a chance to calm down . . .'

But she shook her head sadly. 'My brother is stubborn,' she said. 'I know him too well. Once you cross him, there is no going back. But I will remember you with fondness, Alec. I'm glad I met you.' She stepped forward and impulsively kissed him on the cheek. 'I wish you a good journey to the underworld,' she murmured. She squeezed his hand and then walked quickly away. Alec gazed after her and then touched his cheek where her lips had brushed against it.

He felt a heavy hand on his shoulder and looked up into the impassive face of Tlaloc.

'You come now,' said the warrior, and Alec followed him down the steps. As they walked back across the plaza, Alec could see Chicahua's procession moving slowly through the crowds. Once he thought he saw Tepin looking back over her shoulder, as though searching for him. But then Tlaloc steered him through another entrance and they were heading back towards the prison.

Alec noticed two women coming towards him, their heads bowed. He recognized Conchita and one of Chicahua's wives, the plump woman called Nelli. As they drew closer, Nelli started to speak to Tlaloc, distracting him so that Conchita could talk to Alec.

'How are you?' she asked.

'I've been better,' he admitted.

She glanced at Tlaloc and leaned closer so she could speak in hushed tones. 'And how is Frank?'

'He was fine the last time I saw him.' Alec was puzzled by her manner. She seemed contrite, almost humble, not like herself at all.

'I tried to see him myself, but they would not let me into the prison,' she explained. 'Will you . . . Please will you take a message to him for me?'

'Of course,' said Alec.

'Will you tell him I pray for him?' she whispered.

That was a shock. Alec had somehow never thought of Conchita as somebody who prayed for anything but her own success.

'Of course,' he said.

'Since we are apart I have time to think about things. You know, I treat him badly. I care only about the movie business and I see Frank as . . . a means to an end, you know? But when I see him in the plaza—' She broke off for a moment and Alec was astonished to see tears in her eyes. 'He was in danger, but all he care about was trying to find *me*. It made me realize that he is a good man. A fine man. Always he has done everything for me and I just . . . take it for granted. Will you . . . Alec, will you tell him I love him very much and I will pray for him? Will you tell him that, please?'

Alec nodded. 'I'll . . . I'll try,' he said.

'Thank you,' she said. 'I will say a prayer for you too.'

He nodded. 'Thanks,' he said. 'The way things are going, I may need one.'

Conchita pressed closer to him, and for a moment Alec thought she too was going to kiss him on the cheek – but then he felt her push something into his pocket, and when he slipped his hand in, he felt something cold and hard and realized it was an obsidian dagger. He was about to thank her, but then Tlaloc was dismissing Nelli, pushing her aside rudely before taking

Conchita's arm and pulling her away from Alec. He put a hand on his shoulder and prodded him on along the corridor. The two women bowed respectfully to him and continued in the other direction.

Alec moved on, aware of the dagger in his pocket, thinking how much Conchita had changed in just a couple of days. But then, he decided, there was nothing like a life-or-death experience to make you reassess things. He wondered grimly how he would spend his last few days.

'Master Alec!' said Coates, getting to his feet as Alec stepped into the cell. 'Are you all right? We heard people cheering out there.'

'I'm fine,' said Alec. 'And I've some good news . . . and some bad news.'

'Good news first,' suggested Ethan.

'I've just got us another three days.'

'That's great!' said Frank. 'And what's the bad news?'

'Chicahua isn't my friend any more.'

Of course, everybody wanted to know how he had wangled the extra days, so he was obliged to relate the story, step by step, explaining how he had tricked Chicahua into making the bet. When he had finished, everybody – even the usually sarcastic Nelson – congratulated him on his ingenuity.

'I got to hand it you, kid,' the oil man said, 'that was clever of you.' He shrugged. 'But I have to point out it's just a stay of execution. We're not really any better off.'

Ethan nodded. 'No, but it takes a little of the heat off, I guess. The way things stood, it was do or die – we'd have had to try something tonight, or tomorrow at the very latest. Now maybe we can look out for a good opportunity.'

'Maybe this will help,' said Alec, taking the dagger out of his pocket and handing it to Ethan.

The American grinned. 'It sure will!' He tested the edge of the obsidian with his thumb and managed to draw blood. 'It's sharp enough. Where did you get this, kid?'

'Conchita slipped it to me on the way back here.'

'You saw Conchita?' asked Frank.

'Yes. She . . . she asked me to tell you something.'

'Let me guess,' sneered Nelson. 'Her bath

water's too cold and she was wondering if Frank could slip over and heat it up for her.'

Alec gave him a hostile glare. 'It was nothing like that,' he said. He glanced awkwardly at the others. 'It's kind of personal,' he continued.

He and Frank walked off into the furthest corner and spoke in hushed tones. When Alec had told him everything, Frank had a big smile on his face.

'She really said that?' he whispered. 'That she loved me?'

Alec nodded.

'Then it don't matter what happens to me. I'll die a happy man.'

'Well, let's not say "die" just yet,' Alec told him. 'We've still got a few days to come up with a plan.' They went back to join the others. 'And let's not forget, we've got a weapon now.'

'Not much of a weapon,' said Nelson.

'No, but it's better than nothing,' said Ethan. 'And it's small enough to conceal. As far as a plan goes, all we've come up with is jumping the guards when they bring in some food and then trying to fight our way out to the river.' He glanced at Alec. 'Did you see how many were out there?' he asked.

'Just two men,' Alec told him. 'A jailor and an armed guard.'

'Well, we outnumber them, anyway. If we can get a spear off one of them, we'll have a chance of fighting our way out.'

'I still say it's a dumb idea,' said Nelson. 'We'd be taking on half the city.'

'Not if we try it at night,' reasoned Coates. 'When they're all asleep.'

'But the guards don't come in here at night,' said Alec.

'Then we need to find a way to get them in here,' Frank pointed out. 'Cause a commotion or something.'

Luis laughed. 'Maybe you forgot – Nelson was nearly killing me and they didn't take any notice. They're not stupid, they must realize we're trying to think of ways to escape.'

Everyone lapsed into a thoughtful silence.

'How did Itztli react when he realized that you'd tricked the emperor?' Coates asked Alec.

'He wasn't happy,' he replied. 'He gave me a filthy look and then stormed off. Chicahua said he'd never seen him so angry.'

Coates frowned. 'He's the one that worries me most,' he murmured. 'I only saw him for a short while, but I recognized him for what he was. The kind of man who will let nothing stand in his way.'

Alec nodded. 'I agree. He's a nasty piece of work. But . . . even he wouldn't dare oppose the emperor. Would he?'

Coates didn't answer and everyone desperately tried to think of some escape plan. But the day lengthened into afternoon and then into night, and they had come up with precisely nothing. When the evening meal was delivered, the wooden tray was simply pushed into the room and the door slammed shut again. Clearly the guards weren't taking any chances.

They ate their meagre rations in moody silence and then Ethan announced that he could wait no longer.

'OK, here's how it has to be. Tomorrow morning, when they swing that door open, one of us will be waiting on the other side of it. Frank, maybe you could do it? You just have to grab the edge of the door and pull it wide open. Then I'll go through the doorway with this and cut down anyone who stands in my way.' He lifted the stone knife and made a slashing motion. 'The rest of you will follow hard on my heels, grabbing any weapon you can as we go. We don't stop for anything – not until we get to that river. I'll expect every one of you to back me up. Is that understood?'

Frank scowled. 'What about Conchita?' he asked.

There was an uncomfortable silence.

'If there's any way we can get to her, we'll try,' Ethan promised him. 'But the way I figure it, she's in no real danger for the moment. If we can't reach her now, we'll travel until we find help. Then we'll come back for her and take her back, by force if necessary.'

Frank considered this for a moment and then he nodded.

'OK,' said Ethan. 'Anyone got any other questions?'

Nobody did. So they moved to their respective bunks and settled down to wait.

Chapter Nineteen

The Children of Mictlan

I tztli followed Tlaloc down the stone steps into the dark heart of the step pyramid. Rows of flaming wall torches lit their way. Itztli knew that the leader of the jaguar warriors had been more than a little irritated to be called from his chamber at such a late hour. Not that he would ever dare to express his displeasure. He knew how powerful the high priest was and, though not blessed with the brightest of minds, was always mindful of his own skin.

Itztli had decided that he had brooded over his public humiliation long enough. Once had been bad enough – Chicahua ordering him about like some commoner – but to have the outsider pup ridicule him in the games arena in full view of hundreds of people – that had been the final straw. It was time to act upon the words of the lord of Mictlan himself; to take full control of the situation; to place Colotlán under his rule. But he was also aware that he needed Tlaloc's help. Only with his assistance could Itztli hope to control the army of jaguar warriors who dispensed law and order in the city. But he also suspected that Tlaloc would not easily be persuaded to oppose his emperor so he'd decided to sound him out.

'Tlaloc, you realize that the lord of Mictlan is angry with us?' he said.

Tlaloc glanced over his shoulder. 'No, my lord.'

'But of course he is! Why do you think he has been silent since their arrival? No roaring beneath the earth, no shaking of the land. These outsiders come into our city with their evil magic, and instead of sending them to Mictlan, as he demanded, we allow them to live.'

'Only for a few more days, my lord,' reasoned Tlaloc. 'As I understand it, the emperor promised the boy that if he could—'

Itztli was irritated. 'I know what happened, Tlaloc, I was there!' His voice echoed along the narrow stone passage. 'The boy tricked Chicahua – tricked him like the idiot he is; and yet he still elected to honour the bet. But you do not barter with the god of the underworld. You do not tell him to wait upon your whims. He is to be obeyed without question.'

Tlaloc said nothing and they continued on down the stairs in silence. Then Itztli spoke again.

'What is your opinion of Chicahua?' he asked.

'It is not for me to have an opinion,' said Tlaloc without hesitation. 'He is my emperor.'

'He is a child of twelve summers,' said the high priest scornfully. 'Can he be expected to make important decisions on such matters? Could *you* have decided responsibly when you were his age?'

There was another long pause.

'He is my emperor,' said Tlaloc stubbornly. 'I must obey his every decision. That is the law of our city.'

'And what of me? Would you not obey me if I gave you an order?'

'Of course, my lord, without hesitation. But . . .'

'Yes?'

'The word of my emperor must overrule even your commands.'

Itztli smiled mirthlessly in the darkness and
nodded. It was as he had suspected. Ah well, no
matter . . . 'You are a faithful servant, Tlaloc,' he
observed.

They had reached the golden door and Tlaloc
stood aside and turned away to allow Itztli to
operate the lock, which was shaped in the form
of a golden skull. The high priest swung the
door open and then turned back to look at
him.

'Would you like to see inside this chamber?' he
asked innocently.

Tlaloc spun round in amazement. 'I, my lord?
I . . . do not understand. It is not my place to
enter there. Only the high priests are granted
admission.'

Itztli shrugged his thin shoulders. 'The high
priests and those they decide to take into their
confidence,' he said. 'Come now, surely you
would like to see what few other living men have
ever seen?'

Tlaloc licked his lips; Itztli could see that he
was tempted.

'You honour me, my lord, but . . .'

'Yes?'

'Being allowed to pass through that doorway

– that could not buy my obedience in this matter. I would still have to serve the emperor.'

Itztli allowed himself a hollow laugh. 'Of course!' he murmured. 'My dear Tlaloc, I hope you do not think that I would sink so low as to offer you a bribe? I merely wish to reward you for your many services over the years.'

Tlaloc bowed his head. 'Then I respectfully accept your invitation,' he said.

'Good. Take that torch with you and lead the way.'

Tlaloc lifted a torch from the wall and went inside ahead of Itztli, who turned back to secure the heavy door behind them, then followed the big man down the final flight of steps to the great stone gallery. He heard a gasp of wonder emerge from Tlaloc's lips and thought back to the first time he had been granted access to this magical place: how awe-inspiring it had been! He almost envied Tlaloc the experience of seeing it for the first time.

'My lord, it is . . . incredible,' the warrior whispered.

'Indeed,' said Itztli, staring down into the molten core that lay far below them. 'The gates to Mictlan, the home of the lord of the underworld. Do you feel its power, Tlaloc? Do you not tremble before its majesty?'

Tlaloc nodded. He was gazing down in mute amazement and his dark eyes reflected the red-hot lava below.

'Wait here,' the high priest commanded him. 'I have prayers and invocations to offer.'

He walked slowly round the gallery, aware of the hot stone beneath his sandals. He kept moving until he was standing on the far side of the circle, directly opposite Tlaloc. He leaned on the balcony and gazed down into Mictlan, letting the heat bathe his face, and sought to make contact with Mictlantecuhtli. For a moment he felt resistance; then his vision seemed to cloud and he heard the deep measured tones ringing in his head.

ITZTLI. YOU HAVE RETURNED. WHAT NEWS?

Bad news, Great Lord, replied Itztli's inner voice. *As I feared, the boy made the wrong decision.*

HE DARES TO DENY ME WHAT IS RIGHTFULLY MINE?

My lord, I did warn you. He is a child, he thinks as a child, he acts as a child. Who could expect a boy of such tender years to act responsibly?

DO NOT TRY TO TELL ME MY BUSINESS, ITZTLI.

My lord, I would not! Chicahua has granted the outsiders three more days before allowing the sacrifice — and he has taken the youngest of them into his confidence, treating him as a friend.

A FRIEND? HE HAS NO BUSINESS TO EXTEND THE HAND OF FRIENDSHIP TO ANY OUTSIDER OTHER THAN COYOTL.

I agree, my lord. Especially when the boy has tricked him into granting them more time.

Another long pause. Mictlantecuhtli's voice died down to a bubbling, hissing undertone before rising suddenly again.

YOU HAVE BROUGHT ANOTHER INTO MY PRESENCE! SOMEONE WHO DOES NOT BELONG IN THIS HALLOWED PLACE!

Yes, my lord. I beg forgiveness for this transgression. He is the leader of the jaguar warriors. I need his obedience if I am to carry out our plan successfully. But he obeys the emperor. I thought perhaps — the matter we spoke of before —the children of Mictlan? Those who have already been sacrificed to you . . .

AH YES, MY WARRIORS OF THE DEAD —

YOU WISH ME TO SEND THEM TO YOU. WELL, IT COULD BE DONE. BUT YOU REALIZE, ITZTLI, THAT THERE IS ALWAYS A PRICE TO PAY FOR THEIR SERVICES. THEY CANNOT BE BOUGHT CHEAPLY. YOUR SOUL WILL BELONG TO ME.

My lord, you already have my soul. And if I am to carry out your wishes, if I am to deliver the outsiders to you, then . . .

YES. LET IT BE DONE. OBSERVE.

The lord of Mictlan's voice seemed to fade away, replaced by a louder roar from below. There was movement in the molten rock – a great cloud of grey smoke was slowly billowing up.

'My lord!' It was Tlaloc, calling from the other side of the gallery, sounding apprehensive. 'I think we should leave!'

'No, stay where you are!' Itztli shouted back. 'There is no need for alarm.'

'But the smoke!'

'I said *stay*!'

Now the acrid fog was rising up to the gallery, engulfing them both. Looking across, Itztli could see the figure standing on the balcony, about to panic. And as he gazed, he began to see vague shapes in the smoke beside Tlaloc: a row of figures that quickly began to take form, solidify. Now he could make out their blank staring faces, their wizened grey flesh, the gaping holes in their chests where the hearts had been removed.

Tlaloc suddenly became aware of them. He jerked his head left and right, his eyes bulging in their sockets. He gave a gasp of terror, and for an instant Itztli thought he was about to fling himself into the fire below. The priest knew he could not allow that to happen. He shouted an order:

'Tlaloc, do not move! Stay exactly where you are!'

The man froze like a statue, staring straight ahead, an expression of terror on his brutish face. 'What . . . What are these things, my lord?' he cried. 'They look like . . . men, but . . .'

'Calm, Tlaloc, calm! These are the children of Mictlan, sent to help us in our duty. You need have no fear of them.'

Itztli began to prowl along the gallery, edging past the warriors ranged all the way around the circle – some two or three hundred in all, each armed with a spear or club. They remained unmoving, looking straight ahead as he passed by, their eyes as black and dead as the rest of them, waiting to receive their orders.

In Itztli's mind, the lord of Mictlan's voice rose again, whispering, urging him onwards:

MAKE THIS MAN LIKE THE REST OF YOUR ARMY, ITZTLI. THEN HE IS YOURS TO COMMAND. AND ITZTLI?

Yes, my lord?

DO NOT TARRY LONG. YOU HAVE THEIR SERVICES ONLY DURING THE HOURS OF DARKNESS. BY MORNING THEY MUST RETURN TO ME.

Itztli nodded. He slipped a hand beneath his cloak and felt the familiar handle of the obsidian-bladed dagger.

He walked around the circle, smiling re-assuringly at Tlaloc. The big warrior was shaking like a child, his simple mind unable to deal with something so incredible. He was still staring rigidly ahead, afraid to look into the dead eyes of the creatures that stood on either side of him.

'My lord,' he gasped, 'are they demons?'

'Have no fear,' whispered Itztli. 'They are the departed – those who have gone to meet the lord of Mictlan over the centuries. They are our friends. They wish only to serve us.'

But Tlaloc was shaking his head, sweat streaming down his face. 'This is witchcraft!' he cried. 'I want no part of this. Let me out of here now!'

'Hush, Tlaloc.' Itztli placed a hand on the man's shoulder, steadying him. He slid his right hand free of his cloak, the blade glittering in the glow of the molten rock. 'Have no fear, I shall make everything all right.'

He stepped forward and lifted the blade to Tlaloc's chest in one quick, practised movement. The big man grunted in surprise as Itztli brought the blade up and across; he watched the high priest plunge his other hand into his chest and emerge holding his still beating heart. Tlaloc stared down at it in disbelief but he did not fall. The grey smoke was pouring into the opening in his chest; his flesh began to wither, turning the same dull grey as the smoke. For an instant his body sagged, but then he straightened up again. The light in his eyes glazed over and his expression became blank.

Itztli could feel the man's heart still beating against the palm of his hand. 'Tlaloc, do you know me?' he asked softly.

'I do,' murmured Tlaloc, his voice as dead and grey as his flesh.

'Who must you obey now?'

'You, my lord. Only you.'

'Good.' Itztli returned the dagger to its sheath beneath his cloak. He lifted the heart and flung it down into the fires below. 'Now the lord of Mictlan has your heart,' he said. 'And as long as he has it, you will obey my commands. Do you understand?'

Tlaloc nodded. The high priest turned to survey the figures waiting in a great circle all around him. He lifted his voice so that all might hear his words.

'We go up to the city,' he shouted. 'We go to carry out the bidding of the lord of Mictlan. If anyone opposes you, kill them.'

None of them spoke a word, but as if at a given signal, each turned to his left. Itztli headed for the golden door and his army fell into line behind him, marching with a slow, measured tread as he led them out of the chamber and up the steps to the city.

CHAPTER TWENTY
Rude Awakening

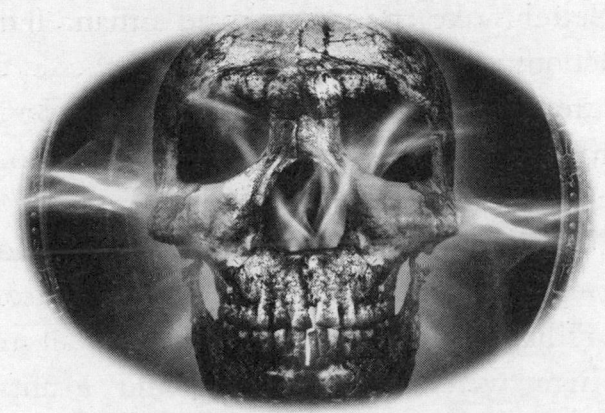

Alec woke to the sound of screaming. He sat up on his bunk and blinked furiously, unsure for a moment where he was. Then the interior of the dark room swam into focus and he looked around. The others were stretched out on their bunks – all except for Ethan, who was standing by the door, as though waiting for somebody. He was holding the stone dagger.

'Ethan, how long have you been standing there?' Alec whispered.

'A while,' muttered Ethan. 'Something's going on outside.'

Alec listened intently for a moment. There it

291

was again – a desperate scream coming from somewhere outside. His blood ran cold. Whatever it was, it didn't sound like good news.

'Better wake the others,' said Ethan. 'I think somebody's coming.'

Sure enough, in the corridor outside they heard footsteps – a slow, measured tread. Alec climbed off his bunk and moved around the cell, shaking the others awake.

'Get ready,' he told them. 'Ethan thinks something's happening.'

There were a few groans and grunts of irritation, but everyone got up and gazed at the door.

'We'll only get one chance,' Ethan told them. 'The moment I grab whoever comes through, I need you to rush him and grab his weapons.'

'What if it's more than one person?' asked Coates.

'Just do your best! We may not get another chance. Quiet now, they're close.'

The marching footsteps were just outside now, and to Alec's befuddled senses it sounded like an army out there. He was getting a bad feeling about this – something had changed, but it was too late to say anything because now the bolts were being slid back. The door creaked open and a figure stepped into the room, silhouetted by the glow of the blazing torch behind him. Alec thought he recognized the tall, muscular shape of Tlaloc. The warrior took a step forward, and at that moment Ethan jumped out from behind the door and leaped forward, driving the stone dagger down between his shoulder blades, burying it to the hilt. Tlaloc grunted but remained upright. The other captives leaped forward to lend a hand, but then they saw Tlaloc clearly and they all stopped in their tracks, staring openmouthed at the creature standing before them.

'What are you waiting for?' bellowed Ethan, pulling the knife free. 'Grab h—'

That was as far as he got. Tlaloc — or the thing that had been Tlaloc — threw back an arm and swatted Ethan aside like an irritating mosquito. Ethan was lifted clear off his feet and thrown back against the wall like a doll. He slammed into it, dislodging chunks of adobe, and slid to the floor, winded. Then more warriors spilled into the room, one of them holding a blazing torch.

Now that Alec could see them in detail, he wanted to cry out in terror. Tlaloc seemed to have shrunk in on himself, his arms and shoulders barely covered with grey flesh through which the bones could be clearly seen. There was a dark opening in his chest where his heart should have been and his eyes were two black, sightless orbs that seemed to stare straight ahead. The handle of the stone dagger jutted from between his shoulder blades, as though it was of no consequence. He took a quick shambling step backwards, bent down and flung out an arm to grab the front of Ethan's shirt. The arm was almost fleshless, but it jerked Ethan back to his feet and propelled him across the room. He fell against a bunk and slumped to the floor. Alec and Coates rushed to help him back to his feet and he turned, baffled, to get his first real look at the creatures that had entered the room.

'Holy Moley!' he said. 'What the hell is going on?'

Alec could come up with nothing that made any sense. He was looking at a row of men who ought to be dead and buried. But they were moving forward now, spears raised to point at the captives' chests.

'The children of Mictlan . . .' Alec heard Luis say, his voice little more than a whisper. Alec was about to ask him to explain, but then Tlaloc spoke, and his voice too was different – a deep, rumbling croak that made the hairs on Alec's neck stand up.

'Come with us,' he said; it wasn't an invitation. Then he lifted a hand and gestured to them impatiently. '*Now!*' Nobody felt like arguing with him.

'Stick together,' Ethan urged the others.

The warriors moved aside and the prisoners stumbled fearfully towards the door. Alec thought about making a run for it in the corridor, but more of the creatures waited for them out there, all armed with spears and clubs, and he knew it was pointless. The warriors closed in around them, and now Alec noticed the smell of them – an overpowering stench of cooked meat that made him gag.

'Where are you taking us?' shouted Nelson, but he got no reply.

They were herded along the corridor while the creatures marched alongside them with a shuffling gait, their blank eyes staring straight ahead.

'Luis,' gasped Alec, 'what are the children of Mictlan?'

The Mexican gave him a strange wild-eyed

look. 'The souls of all the warriors who have been sacrificed to the lord of the underworld,' he said. 'Legend says that they can be called back to do Mictlantecuhtli's bidding, but I thought it was only a story.'

They emerged from the archway at the end of the corridor into a scene of complete devastation. The moonlit streets of Colotlán were in turmoil as hundreds of the undead creatures shambled backwards and forwards, waving their spears and herding the population in the direction of the pyramid. Alec noticed bodies lying in the streets – those who must have tried to oppose the children of Mictlan and had paid the ultimate price.

'Coates,' he gasped, 'I think this is Itztli's doing. I think he means to sacrifice us tonight.'

Coates somehow managed a reassuring smile. 'Take courage, Master Alec,' he said. 'Let's not give them the satisfaction of seeing that we are afraid.'

'The hell with that!' roared Nelson. He turned to the creature nearest to him. 'Listen – I can get you gold, jewels, anything you want. All you have to do is turn your back for a moment and let me go.'

'Shouldn't that be let *us* go?' Luis corrected him.

'It's every man for himself now,' snapped Nelson. He reached out to grab the creature's shoulder. 'Listen to me,' he said. 'I mean it, I'll make any arrangement you want, just let me—' He broke off, looking down in horror as he realized that a chunk of flesh had come away in his hand. 'Oh my God,' he cried. 'Somebody help us!'

Now the dark outline of the step pyramid came into view, and Alec could see that up on its summit, braziers were burning; in front of them stood the silhouetted figures of the priests, dressed in their full regalia.

'I was right,' he murmured. 'They mean to sacrifice us.'

Ethan flashed him a fierce look. 'It ain't over till it's over, kid,' he said.

'Frank!' A familiar voice came from somewhere in the crowd, and Frank looked around desperately until he spotted Conchita, who was being herded forward amongst a crowd of other women. He tried to make his way towards her but was driven back by a casual blow from one of the children of Mictlan.

'Conchita!' he yelled. 'I—' Whatever he said was lost in the sudden roar as the ground beneath their feet shuddered and a great gout of orange flame belched out of the summit of the pyramid. Alec nearly lost his footing and Coates threw out an arm to support him.

'Perfect,' he said. 'As if we didn't have enough to contend with.'

They approached the foot of the pyramid; ahead of them, waiting, were a couple of the dead warriors supporting a familiar figure between them. It was Travers, and Alec could see that a dark crimson stain was spreading across the front of his white cotton robe. He tried to smile at them, but pain turned it into a grimace of agony.

'Good evening . . . my friends,' he gasped. 'I . . . am sorry that your stay in Colotlán could not have been . . . as long as my own.'

'What's happening here?' demanded Ethan.

'Itztli . . . is happening,' said Travers. He pointed up to the summit of the pyramid and now Alec could see the tall figure of the high priest silhouetted against the flames of a brazier. Behind him stood the giant statue of the lord of Mictlan, his grinning skull looking eerily animated in the flickering light of the fire. 'He has . . . taken control. After the ceremony he will proclaim himself emperor.' Travers waved a hand at the pandemonium around them. 'But to invoke the children of Mictlan in this way . . . even I did not think he would resort to such measures.'

'Are you badly injured?' asked Alec.

Travers nodded. 'Fatally so, I fear. When those creatures came to take Chicahua, I opposed them – I grabbed a sword and tried to protect him. I paid the price for my defiance.'

'And Chicahua?' asked Alec.

'Oh . . . I fear his days are numbered. If Itztli does not have him slain, then he and his sister will be thrown into some dungeon to rot. I am sorry you had to see this. Colotlán was once a place . . . to be proud of.'

'Is there nothing you can do to help us?' cried Nelson, his voice ragged with terror. 'There must be some way you can stop this!'

Travers shook his head. 'You must . . . call on your own god,' he said. 'I . . . cannot . . . help you now.'

With that, his head fell forward onto his chest and the two warriors bore him away. Now spears were prodding the captives towards the steps and there was nothing to do but climb them. They began to make their way slowly up to where Itztli waited, his obsidian dagger in his hand.

CHAPTER TWENTY-ONE

Blood Sacrifice

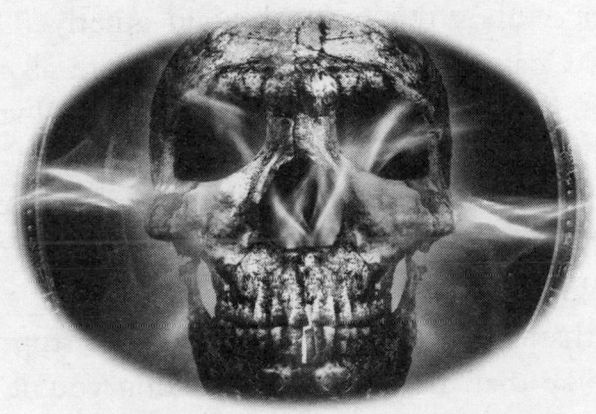

They climbed until they were high above the crowds. Alec felt terror pulsing through him, but also a kind of inner defiance. Coates had told him not to show fear and he was determined to give a good account of himself.

Nelson, on the other hand, was going to pieces. He was whimpering and shaking, his face streaming with sweat. 'This can't be happening,' he kept saying. 'I'm Ulysses T. Nelson.'

Luis studied him for a moment and then said, 'Oh, shut up and try and act like a man.'

Frank was muttering something to himself over and over: 'At least she's safe. At least she's safe.' There was no need to ask who he was talking about.

Alec looked at Coates. 'I may never get a chance to say this again,' he said quietly. 'Thank you, Coates. For putting up with me all these years. I'm sorry for all the awful scrapes I've got us into.'

Coates put a hand on his shoulder. 'It's been a privilege, Master Alec,' he replied. 'And I wouldn't change a thing.'

Ethan glared at them. 'Will you two stop talking like that,' he said. 'I keep telling you, it ain't over till it's over.'

All too soon they had reached the platform at the top of the pyramid. Behind them, spears kept prodding them forward. Alec found himself thinking about his father, feeling sorry that he would almost certainly never know what had become of his only child. He would learn perhaps of an encounter with bandits back in Veracruz, but would have no idea that it had actually ended here in an ancient Aztec city in the middle of the Huasteca Veracruzana.

He heard a voice calling and turned to see Itztli standing by the altar beneath the giant statue of the lord of Mictlan, a cruel smile on his thin face. The god seemed to be observing the sacrifice, grinning down in cruel delight at Alec's fate. Itztli lifted his left hand and gestured to the undead warriors to bring forward the first victim. They began to prod Nelson forward and he cried out.

'Not me!' he screamed. 'Not me, please – somebody else! Somebody else!'

Luis stepped forward and asked him, 'Would you like me to take your place?'

Nelson looked at him, a pathetic expression on his face. 'Yes,' he gasped. 'Please. Please, Luis, I can't . . . it can't be me. Not yet. It's not my time.'

Luis nodded and smiled. He looked at the others. 'Imagine that,' he said with a strange smile. 'Señor Nelson is finally polite enough to say please.' Then he walked calmly across the summit of the pyramid towards the altar. As he did so, the stones shook – another powerful tremor was rippling through the earth and a great gout of flame rushed upwards into the heavens. Itztli stared down at the crowd and shouted something that made them roar their approval. Alec could easily guess the gist of what he had said: that the lord of Mictlan was showing his pleasure at the upcoming sacrifice.

Warriors stepped forward to take Luis; he did not resist them. For a moment he looked across at Alec and gave him a wink. Alec thought that he had never seen a braver man. Next Luis was laid out on the altar and one of the priests ripped open his shirt, revealing his bare chest. He didn't struggle, but stayed absolutely still – though his lips moved. Alec thought that he must be saying a prayer.

Now Itztli lifted the dagger in his hand, drawing another cheer from the assembled crowd, but Alec knew that they were showing approval only because they feared for their own lives.

Itztli stepped closer and looked up at the sky. He shouted something in Nahuatl and then raised the dagger high. At the last instant Alec had to look away. He heard rather than saw what happened next; and when finally he summoned up the courage to look again, Luis's body was gone. There was a puddle of fresh blood at one end of the altar, and a heart was burning on a brazier.

But now Itztli was beckoning again and the spears were prodding Nelson forward. He tried to move but his legs were shaking so much, he could hardly hold himself upright; he was sobbing like a child. Then another tremor shook the stone pyramid and a bigger flame launched itself into the sky, illuminating everything with a red glow. In that instant Nelson's nerve broke. He turned and began to run towards the steps. He rushed down them, fear giving him momentum.

Itztli gave a grimace of irritation and gestured to one of the warriors who stood beside the other captives. The man walked calmly to the top of the steps and lifted his spear to take aim. He paused for a moment and flung it with deadly accuracy. It hit Nelson between the shoulder blades, the tip emerging from his chest. He still kept running, his feet barely touching the stone steps; then he missed his footing and his body went tumbling down into the crowd. The people closed in around him. An instant later, Alec saw a warrior lift the American's head and display it to the crowd, before mounting it on a skull rack.

Alec turned away. He knew now that there was no hope for any of them. When Itztli pointed straight at him, he realized there was no point in putting off the inevitable. He took a step forward but Coates threw out an arm to restrain him.

'No, Master Alec. Let me go in your place!'

A curious sense of calm seemed to settle over Alec. He looked up into the kind face of his valet and thought that he was lucky to have known such a man. Ethan and Frank were trying to struggle forward too, but their guards held them tightly.

'It's pointless delaying it,' Alec told Coates. 'If it's all the same to you, I'd rather get it over with.'

Coates had tears in his eyes. 'Oh, Master Alec,' he said, 'I'm so sorry it has come to this!'

Alec nodded. 'Me too.' He gave Coates a fierce hug and then glanced at Ethan. 'See you in a bit,' he said.

'Don't give 'em the satisfaction of seeing you scared, kid!' yelled Ethan. 'When he lifts that dagger, spit in his eye!'

Alec turned and walked towards the altar. He let the priests take his arms and legs and stretch him out across the cold stone. He felt hands ripping open his shirt but he did not struggle. He thought once again of his father and wished he could have got a message to him somehow. He lay there, staring up at the night sky, and then he felt a curious sensation. The altar beneath him was beginning to shake, but this time there was no sound. It felt as if an incredible power was building, deep in the bowels of the earth.

Itztli seemed oblivious to it. He came forward and smiled mirthlessly down at Alec, his eyes flashing triumphantly. Alec stared back at him. Remembering what Ethan had said, he tried to summon up some spit, but his mouth was parched – but now he realized that the altar was vibrating violently. Then Alec heard a crack and chunks of stone were falling around him. A low murmur coming from within the pyramid quickly built to a roar. Itztli lifted the dagger but paused and turned to look behind and above him. Alec followed his gaze.

The huge statue of Mictlantecuhtli was moving, shuddering as the new tremor grew stronger; and the cheers of the crowd were turning to cries of terror. The altar on which Alec lay suddenly dropped sharply to one side, flinging him off. He rolled, sat upright and turned to look at the statue. A great crack had appeared in one shoulder – a crack that widened as the stone began to shatter. Behind it, a huge wall of orange flame erupted into the night sky, lighting up everything in incredible detail. And then the stone shoulder detached itself, and as

Alec watched, frozen in place, the statue itself began to tilt forward, driven by its own momentum. The other priests began to throw off their masks and run in all directions, but Itztli remained where he was, gazing up at the effigy of his god, which was now falling, falling.

Suddenly an arm grabbed Alec and propelled him towards the steps. He realized it was Ethan – and then his friend was yelling '*Run!*' into his ear, and he rushed down the steps – the steps that seemed to be collapsing beneath his feet. Glancing back, he saw Coates and Frank following him, and just behind them, perilously close, the giant statue was finally toppling over. Alec had one last glimpse of Itztli, dwarfed by the mass of falling rock, and then the statue fell on him, driving him deep into the hollow heart of the pyramid.

Now the air was suddenly thick with ash, and Alec had to cover his mouth and nose with one hand.

The thing that had been Tlaloc barred their path and swung a powerful fist. Ethan ducked the blow, and reaching up, grabbed the handle of the stone dagger that still protruded from between the creature's shoulders. He pulled it free, and as

Tlaloc twisted round to grab at him, he slammed an elbow into his head and sent him sprawling down the steps in front of them, his limbs breaking off as he fell.

'Come on!' yelled Ethan, and he led the way down the steps, slashing with the stone dagger at anyone who opposed him. The others followed hard on his heels.

They started to run through a confusion of screaming, terrified people. Frank veered away from the others for a few moments and then reappeared, dragging Conchita behind him. Another of Mictlan's dead barred their way, and Ethan aimed a punch at it, sending it tumbling backwards.

They emerged from the blanket of ash into an open space where the air was clearer. Here they hesitated for a moment, staring frantically this way and that, unsure which direction to take. Alec turned to look back at the pyramid and gave a gasp of astonishment, for now he saw that the entire edifice was tumbling inwards on itself as it fell into an ever-widening chasm – a chasm that spread closer and closer. An undead warrior came running towards him, an obsidian-tipped club raised to strike, but then the crack in the earth found his running feet and he dropped into the abyss.

'Ethan!' yelled Alec.

Ethan looked, saw, nodded. 'Come on!' he cried. 'This way!'

He took off, racing down a narrow alleyway, and the others followed. Alec was horribly aware that, as they ran, the adobe walls behind were crashing to the ground. They turned a corner and saw the jetty ahead of them. A couple of women were helping two children into a dugout canoe. They turned, saw Alec and waved at him. Chicahua and Tepin were being taken to safety by Nelli and another of the wives. As they watched, the women started paddling away upriver – Alec wondered where they were making for. Their lives would certainly be very different from now on – he was sure of that. Chicahua looked stunned by what was happening. He lifted a chubby hand to wave and Alec saw that he was indeed nothing more than a frightened twelve-year-old boy. Tepin stood up and stared wistfully back; for a moment Alec thought she was going to jump out of the canoe and swim back to join him . . . But then she lowered her gaze and sat down beside her brother, throwing an arm protectively around his shoulders.

There was no time to ponder the moment – dark shapes were shambling towards the docks. Ethan ran over to the biggest canoe and urged the others to follow. Frank helped Conchita in, then jumped in beside her, followed by Alec and Coates. Meanwhile Ethan bent down to untie the mooring rope. But behind him, two dark figures were racing along the wooden jetty to intercept them.

Alec looked around frantically and his eyes lit upon a pile of fishing nets in the bottom of the boat, the ends weighted with heavy stones. Snatching up one of the nets, he whirled it round above his head several times to gain momentum. The nearest figure was just raising his spear to plunge it into Ethan's back as he struggled with the mooring rope, oblivious to the threat, when Alec threw the net, hoping against hope that his aim was true. It flew through the air, wrapped itself around the head of the warrior and threw him backwards into his companion, knocking both of them to the ground.

Surprised, Ethan turned to look at the struggling figures on the jetty.

'Come on!' Alec urged him.

Ethan leaped into the canoe, and he and Frank both grabbed paddles, forcing it through the water with all their might, heading for the middle of the river where the current was strongest. In the stern, Alec turned to gaze back at the destruction behind them. Flames and ash were spewing up into the sky. There was now nothing to be seen of the great step pyramid, and as far as Alec could see, nothing to tell the world that it had ever been there.

Then he noticed an undead warrior with a bow standing on the jetty. As Alec watched, the creature nocked an arrow, aiming for the boat.

'Watch out, everyone!' he yelled, and was about to throw himself down when something struck him in the left shoulder and flung him onto his back. He lay in the bottom of the canoe, gasping for breath, and then turned his head to see the long shaft of an arrow sticking out of his shoulder.

'Master Alec!' Coates was kneeling beside him to examine the injury. 'Oh my lord, Mr Wade, he's been shot.'

'I'm all right,' gasped Alec. It was true, he couldn't feel a thing – not until he tried to move, and then it was like somebody had poured acid into his shoulder. He gritted his teeth against the pain. A second arrow splashed down into the water a short distance behind the boat and Alec realized that they must be moving out of range. He looked up at Coates and forced a grin. 'Don't worry,' he said. 'I'm fine.'

Now Ethan came scrambling back to his side, a grave expression on his face. He lifted Alec into a sitting position. 'It's gone right through,' he said. 'Alec, you're going to have to brace yourself.'

Alec nodded. Ethan held the shaft end of the arrow and then quickly and decisively snapped off the feathered part. He looked at Alec. 'You OK?'

Alec nodded, but he was aware of the sweat pouring down his face.

'Now, I've got to pull the business end of this thing out of your shoulder,' he said. 'I'll try and be as quick as I can.'

Alec nodded. He was scared, but even more afraid of leaving the arrow inside him. He knew from his research that many of the jungle tribes liked to poison the tips of their arrows. 'Do what you have to,' he said grimly.

Coates held him while Ethan moved behind

him, saying, 'Take a deep breath. I'm going to count to three. One . . . two . . .'

But he pulled on two, and Alec felt the worst pain he had ever experienced in his life. It was like fire passing through his flesh. A redness seemed to swell in his head, and then it turned into the deepest black. He let out a long sigh and slipped into unconsciousness.

Chapter Twenty-two

Downriver

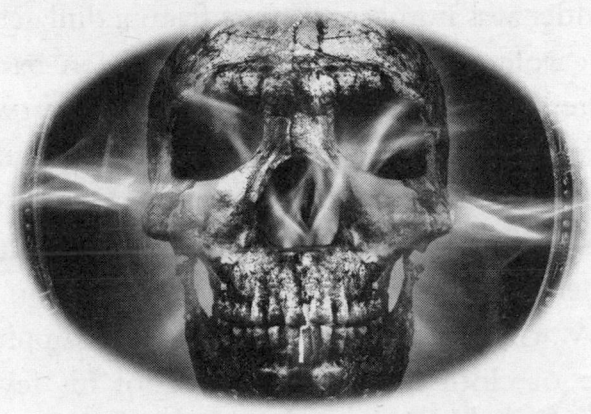

They had been drifting downriver for several days now. Alec lay in the stern of the canoe, covered with an old blanket. He couldn't seem to stop shivering, though the sweat poured down his face.

He was dying – he was convinced of it. He knew this from the way Ethan and Coates kept going off into a huddle, whispering to each other. There had been something on the head of that arrow – something that was slowly working its way into his system. His body was shutting itself down, bit by bit. How ironic, he thought, to have come so close to death up on the pyramid, only to be caught by a last arrow when he had almost escaped from the clutches of the city.

He wasn't in too much pain. The whole of his shoulder was numb, and apart from a dull ache in his temples he might almost have been back in England, enjoying a lazy day on the river while his father rowed him along the Thames.

The others took turns to sit with him, even Conchita, who after the ordeal in Colotlán seemed to have emerged a changed person. She was warm and caring, continuously dipping a piece of cloth in the river to cool his fevered brow. She told him about her life as a young chorus girl in Acapulco; and how she had mistakenly eaten dog back in the royal palace. He would have laughed at her stories if he'd had the strength.

The men caught fish as they went downstream, using the other net in the bottom of the boat; and every evening they found a place to pull into the riverbank, so they could build a fire and cook their evening meal. Starting a fire with no matches called for every bit of ingenuity, particularly as they no longer had Luis's survival skills to call on. They had to twirl a length of dry wood between the palms of their hands, the end of it thrust into a notch cut into a piece of flat wood. The resulting friction eventually provided enough heat to ignite a couple of scraps of bark, but it took for ever and sometimes it was totally dark before the fish was cooking.

Alec tried eating, knowing how important it was to keep up his strength, but within a few minutes he just vomited up everything he ate, and as the days slipped by, he grew steadily weaker. They saw no other people on the thickly forested banks of the river – just the occasional bird or some prowling cat slinking through the undergrowth.

One afternoon, when Coates was sitting beside him, Alec decided it was time to speak of what was on his mind. 'Coates,' he said, 'when you get back to Veracruz—'

'When *we* get back,' Coates corrected him.

'I want you to tell my father that I'm sorry – for being so reckless.'

'You'll be able to tell him that yourself,' Coates assured him.

Alec shook his head and then groaned at the discomfort this caused him. 'I think we both know I'm done for,' he said. 'I want you to tell Father that it was all my fault. If I hadn't made you come and look at that Olmec head, we'd be back in Veracruz, safe and sound.'

'Master Alec, you mustn't talk like that!' Alec was shocked to see that the valet's eyes were filling with tears. 'You're going to be just fine. It can't be long now before we reach a village and then . . . then we'll be able to get you some proper medical attention. You just have to hold on a little while longer.'

But Alec could feel himself slipping away. He was so tired, so very tired . . . He closed his eyes and Coates's voice became a strange booming sound that seemed to be coming from a long way off.

He opened his eyes again. It was night time, but the boat was still on the water. He wondered why they hadn't put in to the bank. A gentle hand was stroking his hair and he looked up to see that it was his mother, Hannah. He was amazed to see her here. Wasn't she dead, a year or more? She smiled down at him, and all his cares seemed to drift away.

'What are you doing here?' he asked her, puzzled.

'Can't a mother spend a little time with her son?' she asked him.

'Yes, but . . . aren't you . . . ?' He realized what must be happening and smiled up at her. 'I thought . . . I thought I'd never see you again,' he said.

'But Alec, I'm *always* with you. Didn't you know that? Every step you take, I'm watching you. And I wanted you to know how proud I am of you.'

'Proud?' He felt his own eyes misting with tears. 'I don't know what there is to be proud of. I made a mess of everything. I got everybody into such an awful scrape . . .'

'Not a scrape,' said Hannah, shaking her head. 'An adventure, Alec. And Lord knows, there's precious little of that left in the world.'

He forced a smile. 'You always let me get away with things,' he said.

'I think you're confusing me with your father,' she whispered. She lifted her head and Alec saw that her face was suddenly lit up. They were moving towards the riverbank now and there was a light blazing, so bright it made him squint. There was a commotion at the water's edge: he could hear somebody shouting urgently. It sounded like Ethan.

'What's happening?' he asked.

Hannah turned and smiled down at him. 'Nothing for you to worry about,' she assured him. 'You rest now.'

His eyelids felt like lead weights and sleep was dragging at him, pulling him back down into darkness, but there was one more question that he had to ask.

'Am I dead?' he gasped, but no answer came to him and he could fight it no longer. He slipped down into blackness.

CHAPTER TWENTY-THREE
Safe Haven

Alec opened his eyes. His mother was still there, her hand stroking his hair. He smiled up at her but she seemed to shimmer like an apparition, and then she became somebody completely different. Conchita. She was looking down at him with a puzzled expression.

'Why you keep calling me Mother?' she asked.

Alec gazed up at her for a moment and then turned to look at his surroundings. He saw that he was lying in a proper bed under a thatched roof in what appeared to be a crude adobe dwelling. Questions came to him in a confused jumble, and he could barely manage to get the first of them out: 'Where . . . ? What . . . ? How . . . ?'

'Shush. You're still very weak,' Conchita told him. 'Here, have some of this.' She lifted a glass to his lips. The cool, clear water slipped down his throat, instantly restoring some of his vitality. He let it go down and was pleased to note that he didn't feel like throwing it straight up again. A good sign.

'Where are we?' he asked. He reached out a hand to touch his shoulder and discovered that it was tightly bandaged.

'We found a village,' Conchita told him. 'We only just got you here in time. You've been asleep for three days.'

'Three days!' Alec tried to sit up but found he didn't have the strength. 'My mother . . . my mother was here . . . wasn't she?'

'You mus' have been dreaming,' said Conchita. She smiled down at him. 'Ethan tol' me about your mother. She sounds like a very special lady.'

Alec nodded. 'It was . . . as though she was with me,' he murmured. He looked around again. 'I could have sworn . . .' He shook his head. 'Tell me about the village.'

'It's a missionary outpost,' said a familiar voice;

and looking up, Alec saw that Ethan and Coates had just come in through the open doorway. Both of them were smiling with what looked suspiciously like relief. They came and stood beside the bed. 'You sure gave us a scare, kid,' said Ethan. 'You were pretty out of it. Father Ortega told me that the tribes around here have a nasty habit of scraping stuff off the back of a toad and dipping their arrowheads in it. We can't be sure, but we think that's what might have happened to you.'

'Father Ortega?' said Alec.

'A Catholic missionary,' explained Coates. 'He's been living in this village for a couple of years now, bringing Christianity to the people of the rainforest. We'd just about given up on you, and then we saw his lights burning on the riverbank.'

Alec nodded. 'I think I remember the lights,' he said. He gestured to Conchita. 'Can I have a little more water, please?'

'Sure you can. In a little while I'll bring you some soup.' She leaned closer. 'Don' worry – I checked. There's no dog in it.'

Alec managed a weak chuckle.

'Of course,' said Ethan, 'we didn't know if it

was a friendly village, but we knew if we didn't stop here, it would be the end of the line for you.' He shrugged. 'The gamble paid off. Father Ortega is also a pretty good doctor. He fixed you up. The first twenty-four hours were touch and go, but it looks like you're on the mend. He figures you'll be back on your feet in a couple of days.'

Somebody else came into the hut. It was Frank. A huge grin spread across his face when he saw Alec. 'Oh good!' he said. 'You're feelin' better, are you?'

'Yes, thanks,' said Alec. He looked at Coates. 'So how far are we from civilization?'

Coates smiled. 'Still a fair distance. But the good news is that in three days' time there's a steamboat calling here to drop off provisions. We'll be able to grab a ride with them back to a place called Salinas. And from there, we'll be able to pick up another boat to Veracruz.'

'*And* we'll be able to telegraph your father – tell him that you're safe,' added Ethan.

Frank moved closer to the bed. 'And I might be able to get a telegraph to Louis B. Mayer – tell him why Conchita never turned up for that screen test.'

Everyone looked at him.

'He might still be in Tonala,' protested Frank. 'And when I tell him my idea for a new scenario, he's going to fall about.' He lifted his hands to frame an imaginary title. 'Conchita Velez in *City of the Aztecs*!' he cried. 'What d'you think of that?'

'Sounds good,' said Alec. 'If a little far-fetched.'

They all laughed.

Ethan looked slyly at Frank. 'You going to tell Alec about your other news?' he asked.

Frank smiled. 'Why not?' He reached across the bed and took Conchita's hand. 'Miss Velez has done me the great honour of agreeing to be my wife,' he said.

Alec was delighted. 'That's . . . wonderful news . . . But' – he looked at Conchita – 'don't you already have a husband?'

She chuckled. 'I don' think it is official when he is only twelve years old,' she said.

'Well, Alec, I'm glad you're on the mend,' said Frank. 'Now, if I can drag my fiancée away for a moment, I've a few things I need to discuss with her.'

'Of course,' said Alec.

Conchita smiled down at him. 'I come and see

you later,' she said. 'I bring you that soup. You know, Frank and me, we have already decided we want you to be our pageboy. I hope you will say yes.' She leaned down and kissed him gently on the cheek. Then she and Frank went out hand in hand.

'Pageboy?' muttered Alec.

'Yes, Master Alec,' said Coates with a malicious smile. 'I believe it involves wearing a rather fetching velvet suit.'

Alec grimaced. 'I suppose I'll have to say yes . . .'

'I'm afraid so.'

Ethan was gazing after Conchita. 'Can you believe the change in that dame?' he said. 'A few days ago she had the disposition of a grizzly bear sitting on a cactus. Now she's a regular sweetie pie. I guess there's nothing like being in fear for your life for making you realize what's really important.' He turned back to Alec. 'Well, kid, looks like we made it out of there in one piece. Didn't I keep telling you it ain't over till it's over. All you need to do for the next few days is rest up and get your strength back.'

'And then go back and face my father,' said Alec apprehensively.

'Oh, I'm sure you'll be all right,' said Coates. 'Especially when we tell him how close he came to losing you.'

Alec could feel sleep overtaking him again, but there were still a few questions he needed answers to. 'And what do we tell Father when we see him again? About . . . about what happened to us,' he asked.

'The bare minimum,' said Coates. 'We crashed in the jungle . . .'

'We came up against hostile Indian tribes,' added Ethan.

'And after making a desperate run for it,' concluded Coates, 'we escaped with our lives.'

'And . . . Colotlán?' murmured Alec.

'There's no such place any more,' said Ethan. 'As I remember, it just kind of . . . fell into a hole in the ground.'

'And the . . . the children of . . . Mictlan?'

Ethan and Coates exchanged looks of exaggerated innocence, then turned back to look at Alec. 'The *what*?' they said together.

Alec smiled and nodded. Sleep was crowding in on him again, and try as he might, he could resist it no longer. But he was happy to rest now. All in all, he felt he'd earned it.

EYE OF THE SERPENT
by Philip Caveney

Alec Devlin's adventures begin in this fast,
furious and sometimes terrifying adventure.

Egypt 1923.

Fifteen-year-old Alec Devlin is on his way to the Valley of the
Kings to spend his summer holidays working on his Uncle
Will's archaeological dig. It's not the first time he's spent his
summer this way . . . but this year things are different.

Uncle Will and his young assistant, Tom Hinton,
have recently made an amazing discovery – an ancient tomb
hidden deep below the earth. But only hours after opening its
doors, Uncle Will falls mysteriously ill and Tom seems
to have disappeared without trace.

Alec sets about unravelling the tomb's mysteries. Seemingly
harmless animals have turned into rabid killers . . . long
dead mummies are rising from their tombs . . . and Alec
must confront a terror that has waited three
thousand years to be reborn.

RED FOX
ISBN 978 1 862 30608 0

Sebastian Darke: Prince Of Fools
By Philip Caveney

Sebastian Darke has the world on his narrow shoulders.
The son of a human father and an elvish mother,
he is deperately trying to become the family bread
winner and has taken on his late father's
job – celebrated jester, *Prince of Fools*.

Trouble is, Sebastian can't tell a joke to save his
life. Dressed in his father's clothes and accompanied
by his talking (and endlessly complaining) buffalope,
Max, he sets off for the fabled city of Keladon,
where he hopes to be appointed court jester to
King Septimus. On the way he encounters a tiny
but powerful warrior called Cornelius; blood-thirsty
Brigands and enough perils to make him wonder
why he ever decided to leave home.

A hilarious and swashbuckling adventure!

RED FOX
ISBN 978 1 862 30251 8

Sebastian Darke: Prince of Pirates
by Philip Caveney

Sebastian, Max and Cornelius are ready for another adventure and heading to the bustling port of Ramalat. Once there they intend to embark on a perilous sea journey in search of the fabled lost treasure of the pirate King, Captain Calinestra.

But when they finally reach Ramalat, a feisty female sea captain; an infamous young pirate; ravenous sea creatures, giant lizards; furious sea battles and breathtaking action await them.

Will they discover the lost treasure? Will Sebastian live to tell the tale? Will Cornelius be beaten in armed combat? And will Max EVER stop moaning?

RED FOX
ISBN 978 1 862 30257 0